The Professor and the Puzzle

WITHDRAWN
Franklin LRC

Read all the mysteries in the

NANCY DREW DIARIES

❧

Benjamin Franklin School
Learning Resource Center

Nancy Drew

DIARIES™

School Dist. 64
164 S. Prospect Ave.
Park Ridge, IL 60068

The Professor and the Puzzle

#15

CAROLYN KEENE

Aladdin

NEW YORK   LONDON   TORONTO   SYDNEY   NEW DELHI

If you purchased this book without a cover, you should be aware that this book is stolen property.
It was reported as "unsold and destroyed" to the publisher, and neither the author
nor the publisher has received any payment for this "stripped book."

This book is a work of fiction. Any references to historical events, real people,
or real places are used fictitiously. Other names, characters, places, and events are products of the
author's imagination, and any resemblance to actual events or places or persons,
living or dead, is entirely coincidental.

ALADDIN

An imprint of Simon & Schuster Children's Publishing Division
1230 Avenue of the Americas, New York, New York 10020
First Aladdin paperback edition August 2017
Text copyright © 2017 by Simon & Schuster, Inc.
Cover illustration copyright © 2017 by Erin McGuire
Also available in an Aladdin hardcover edition.
All rights reserved, including the right of reproduction in whole or in part in any form.
ALADDIN and related logo are registered trademarks of Simon & Schuster, Inc.
NANCY DREW, NANCY DREW DIARIES, and related logo are
trademarks of Simon & Schuster, Inc.
For information about special discounts for bulk purchases, please contact
Simon & Schuster Special Sales at 1-866-506-1949 or business@simonandschuster.com.
The Simon & Schuster Speakers Bureau can bring authors to your live event.
For more information or to book an event contact the Simon & Schuster Speakers Bureau
at 1-866-248-3049 or visit our website at www.simonspeakers.com.
Cover designed by Karin Paprocki
Interior designed by Mike Rosamilia
The text of this book was set in Adobe Caslon Pro.
Manufactured in the United States of America 0717 OFF
2 4 6 8 10 9 7 5 3 1
Library of Congress Control Number 2017939253
ISBN 978-1-4814-8544-9 (hc)
ISBN 978-1-4814-8543-2 (pbk)
ISBN 978-1-4814-8545-6 (eBook)

Contents

Dear Diary,

TALK ABOUT A BLAST FROM THE PAST!
My old pal Iris Pappas called me the other day—
she and I haven't spoken in years. Her father is the
president of Oracle College, and the two of them
live in the president's mansion on campus. We got a
chance to catch up, but that's not even the best part:
she invited the girls and me to the mansion for a big
costume party! It's Greek-themed, and George, Bess,
and I have already started planning our costumes.
I've never been to a party like this one. I'm certain it's
going to be a night to remember!

The Professor and the Puzzle

CHAPTER ONE

The Oncoming Storm

IT WAS ONLY THREE O'CLOCK IN THE afternoon, but the sky over Oracle College looked as dark as midnight. The tiny campus, nestled in the mountains outside River Heights, seemed to huddle more closely under its cover of trees as a driving rain began to fall, causing students and professors alike to race for shelter.

Peeking out the window of my parked car, I winced as a finger of lightning flashed across the sky, followed closely by a deafening crack of thunder. "It looks like Zeus himself is planning on attending the gala tonight," I mused, pulling the hood of my raincoat tight around my face.

Next to me in the passenger seat, my friend Bess Marvin was pulling a compact umbrella out of her purse. "If he did, he wouldn't even be the most famous person there," she joked. "I still can't believe we get to attend the annual Greek Gala! Anyone who's anyone in River Heights is invited. Leave it to you, Nancy, to be friends with the right people and get us on the guest list!"

I smiled. "Yeah, Iris and I go way back." I remembered fondly those days, many years ago, when Iris Pappas and I played together in the backyard of my house, while Dr. Pappas and my dad talked together on the porch. The two men were fraternity brothers from their college days, and so Iris and I became natural friends. Now Giorgio Pappas was the president of Oracle College, and the host of the annual Greek Gala. After a little cajoling, Iris had convinced her father to extend an invitation to me and my friends.

"Well, what are we waiting for?" George Fayne, Bess's cousin and my other best friend, said from the backseat. "Let's go!"

Bess and I glanced glumly out the windshield at the fat drops of rain pouring down in rivulets. "But it's so . . . ," Bess began.

"Wet," I finished.

George rolled her eyes. "Ugh, come on! A little rain never hurt anybody. To the president's mansion!" And with that, she slung her duffel bag around across her shoulders, flung open the car door, and leaped into the storm.

Bess and I watched her go. "But she didn't have a raincoat *or* an umbrella!" Bess exclaimed.

I smirked. "Well, like she said, a little rain never hurt anybody."

After a mad dash through the campus, Bess and I came to a wide, cobblestoned pathway that led up to the president's mansion. Surrounded by manicured hedgerows, blooming pink hydrangeas, and hundred-year-old oak trees whose leaves were just beginning to change into their autumn colors, the gray stone residence was abuzz with activity, as caterers and other household staff carried in everything they needed for the evening's festivities.

We found George standing just under the colonnade, looking like a drowned rat, with her short, dark brown hair and clothes dripping into a growing puddle around her feet. I stifled a laugh as George eyed us sheepishly. "Okay," she said. "So maybe it was more than just a *little* rain. . . ."

Laughing, I took off my raincoat and tried to shake off some of the water. Bess did the same with her little umbrella.

"Nancy! Oh, you made it!"

I turned toward the familiar voice to see the Amazonian figure of Iris Pappas striding toward me. She swept me into one of her trademark rib-crushing hugs, and then stood back to give me a once-over. "Look at you! You look fabulous, babe."

"Me?" I scoffed, fingering a sodden lock of red hair

that had escaped my hood. "Between the two of us, *you're* the glamour girl, not me! I bet you made that dress, didn't you?"

"This old thing?" Iris purred. She did a little twirl, which caused the emerald-green, jewel-studded wrap dress she was wearing to flare out around her. The color beautifully set off Iris's long chestnut hair and olive complexion. "You like it? It's part of a new line I'm working on for one of my merchandising classes. Catwalk-worthy fashions for tall, curvy ladies—at a reasonable price, of course."

I chuckled. Iris was pursuing a degree in fashion merchandising from Oracle, a fact that surprised no one. Iris might as well have been born with a sewing needle in her hand.

"I don't like it—I love it!" Bess exclaimed. "Can you make one in my size?"

Iris turned to the bubbly, blond, blue-eyed girl and said, "You must be Bess. I've heard so much about you. Given your own passion for fashion, I can't wait to see what costume you've got planned for tonight!"

"Oh," Bess breathed, her eyes sparkling with excitement. "It's really good, Iris, it's a—"

"H-hey!" George interrupted. "Zip it! It's a surprise, remember? I didn't keep my costume a secret for three weeks just to have you spilling the beans right before the gala!"

Bess wilted. "Okay, okay. You're right. I'm just so excited! How often do you get to dress like a Greek goddess at the most well-attended party of the year?"

I couldn't blame Bess for her enthusiasm. The Greek Gala was an annual event where wealthy and influential donors to the college were invited to dress up as their favorite characters from Greek mythology. Iris's father dreamed up the idea when he became president of Oracle five years ago and needed a way to boost the college's flagging enrollment numbers and donations. Being of Greek descent himself, and an ex-classics professor at Oracle, Dr. Pappas thought that a Greek-themed costume party might be just the thing to liven up the boring old cocktail parties his predecessor used to host. And it was. Within a year, Oracle saw its enrollment—and its bank account—start to grow. So the gala, with each passing year, grew too.

"Where are my manners?" Iris exclaimed. "Here I am talking shop, and your friend is freezing to death on my doorstep. It's George, right?"

"Y-yup," George answered, her teeth chattering. She took a moment to shake some of the excess water off her jeans and squeeze a few drops out of her gray graphic tee. Unlike her stylish cousin Bess, George tended to dress for comfort—though right now she was probably anything but comfortable. "Sorry about the puddle, Iris. I may have underestimated the weather a b-bit."

"Let's get you into some dry clothes," Iris said, ushering us inside the front door. "I'm sure I can get the caterers to whip up a few mugs of hot chocolate, too."

Inside the mansion, we were greeted by a sumptuous entry hall painted in sapphire blue and hung with oil portraits of past college presidents. Catering staff swarmed across the polished wooden floors, carrying blue vases bursting with white lilies, decorative columns, and silver serving dishes. A large table stood in the center of the room, covered in tiny white cards. I saw that each card was inscribed with a hand-written name, and I scanned the table to find my own. *Miss Nancy Drew*, the card read, and then beneath that, *Polyhymnia*. Before I could ask what the word meant, a booming voice broke through the low hum of voices like a crack of thunder. "My, my!" the voice said. "How you've grown, *mikrí alepoú*!"

I grinned and glanced up from the table to see the figure of Giorgio Pappas striding toward me. Like his daughter, Dr. Pappas cut an imposing fig-ure, his steel-gray suit straining to contain his barrel chest and wide shoulders. His curly, raven-black hair and beard framed an angular, noble face that always reminded me of one of those marble busts from Greek antiquity.

"Mikri-what?" George whispered in my ear.

"*Mikrí alepoú*," I whispered back. "Little Fox. It was his nickname for me when I was a little girl." I walked forward a few steps before being enveloped in another viselike embrace. "It's so good to see you again, Papa George," I managed to squeak out once I could breathe again.

"Still getting yourself into all manner of trouble, I expect?" Dr. Pappas asked, his dark eyes sparkling.

"You could say that," I replied. Dr. Pappas was referring to my reputation as an amateur sleuth, which had gotten me into more than a few tight spots over the years.

"Do you remember 'The Case of the Missing Cat'?" Dr. Pappas said with a smirk. "It took the grounds-keeper's tallest ladder to get you girls out of that tree!"

Bess and George laughed. "Yes, well," I muttered, blushing furiously. "I can't say it was my finest hour. But in my defense, I was only eight. I hadn't yet mastered all my powers of deduction."

"Did you ever find the cat?" George asked, curious.

I bit my lip. "He was sleeping under the couch. Not much of a mystery, as it turned out."

"Ah, yes," Dr. Pappas said. "Argus—he was a good old tomcat. All eyes, he was. Guarded that house from vermin like it was his life's calling." Suddenly a look of terrible sadness crinkled the man's face.

"Dad?" Iris said, after a moment's silence. "Everything okay?"

Dr. Pappas started, like someone just woken from a dream. "What's that, dear? Oh—fine, fine, of course. Just a lot on my mind. You'll understand, girls, if I excuse myself to assist the staff with the final preparations. See you all tonight!" With a crisp nod, Dr. Pappas departed, a gaggle of caterers trailing behind, carrying armfuls of decorations and peppering him with questions.

I stared after him, puzzled. "What was that all about, Iris? I know he really adored Argus, but—"

"It's not the cat," Iris said with a sigh. "He's still broken up about losing Cameron Walsh a few months ago. Dr. Walsh was the one who gave Argus his name, you know. They found him as a kitten behind one of the academic buildings one night, and Dad decided to keep him."

"Who's Cameron Walsh?" Bess asked.

"The chair of classics here at Oracle," Iris answered.

"He was Dad's good friend and mentor for many years. They worked together continuously until Dad became president of the university. Dr. Walsh was ill for a long time and finally passed away three months ago. He kept working up until the very end. Dad was devastated. He still hasn't been able to bring himself to name a replacement."

"How awful," Bess said. "Poor Dr. Pappas."

"I'm so sorry, Iris," I added. "I had no idea. Is there anything we can do?"

Iris squeezed my shoulder. "How sweet of you to ask. But the best thing you can do is have a wonderful time at the gala tonight! Seeing your smiling faces will drive away the dark clouds hanging over Dad's head for sure."

Outside, a bolt of lightning flooded the room with a flash of white light. "If only they could drive away the ones up in the sky as well!" George grumbled.

Iris put her hands on her hips, glancing out onto the rain-soaked lawn beyond. "Ugh, this weather!" she exclaimed. "I just hope we don't lose the power tonight.

Dad said that the caterers have brought in cases of tea lights and electric candles, just in case."

"Oh, how romantic!" Bess gasped.

George rolled her eyes. "Only you could find the romance in a widespread power outage," she said.

"And only *you* would walk out into a torrential downpour with no umbrella! If you don't get out of those wet clothes soon, you're going to be stuck in bed with a box of tissues tonight."

George glanced down at her sopping T-shirt and jeans and sighed. "I guess you're right," she said. "Iris, can you tell us where our rooms are?"

After giving us directions to the bedrooms upstairs, Iris added, "And I'd love to give you girls a tour of the mansion, when you've got a chance."

"That sounds great, but I really need to get started on my hair," Bess replied. "It's a bit, um, involved."

Iris turned to me. "How about you, Nancy? Are you game?"

"Sure!" I said. "I should have plenty of time to get dressed before the gala. Let's go!"

While Bess and George—her shoes squishing with every step—headed upstairs, I followed Iris deeper into the house, leaving my luggage and wet coat at the foot of the stairs. It was a wondrous place, filled with art and history, and more books than I'd seen in any one place. "If you liked the library," Iris said after we had been exploring for a while, "wait until you see the ballroom."

With a dramatic flourish, she threw open a door that led straight into the grand ballroom, where tonight's Greek Gala was to take place. I gasped as I got a glimpse of the two-story circular chamber, with its ivy-strewn white columns, its colorful frescoes of dancing Greek figures, and the magnificent crystal chandelier hanging from the ceiling high above. An elegant spiral staircase led to a second-floor balcony level, which encircled the ballroom, edged with metal railings. On one side, the balcony jutted out over the waxed wooden dance floor. I could just imagine someone presiding over the party from up on that balcony, like a king overseeing his subjects.

On the other side of the room from the dance floor, dining tables dressed in midnight blue and silver were placed, with ten chairs set around them. In the center of each stood a two-foot-tall white statue, each one different from the next. Curious, I approached the closest one for a better look. It depicted a robed woman leaning on a column, her chin perched on one hand, and her face set in an expression of deep thought. The card at the base of the statue read, *Polyhymnia*.

"Hey," I said to Iris, "this is the name on my seating card. Who is she?"

"One of the Muses," Iris replied. "I thought it would be a fun way to identify the different tables, since there are nine of them. Dad's not the only one who knows a thing or two about ancient Greece." She winked. "Polyhymnia is the patron of religious hymn, prayer, and sacred dance." She gave me a playful nudge. "Dad doesn't let me do much of anything for the gala—he says I shouldn't be distracted from my studies—but he did let me choose where you guys would sit. I put you at this table because I thought she looked a lot like you did when we were kids and you had some problem in your head you were trying to solve."

I glanced back at the face of the statue and chuckled. Polyhymnia, with her furrowed brows and her mouth pressed into a serious line, really did look like she was in the middle of a hard-to-crack case. "Guilty as charged," I said.

"Well, let's hope that tonight, the most you'll have to puzzle out is whether you want the chicken or the fish!" Iris chuckled.

As we walked around the room, admiring the decor, I felt something crunch underneath my shoe. I lifted my foot to see that I'd stepped in a pile of small, clay-colored fragments scattered on the floor. I rubbed a few of the fragments between my fingers—they were a bit glossy on one side, almost like paint. "What's this, I wonder?" I asked, almost to myself.

Iris leaned over to look. "Oh, probably just some grit the caterers forgot to sweep up when they cleaned the room. Don't worry about it."

I dusted off my shoe and we went on. Iris looked

around the room with pride before squeezing my hand inside her larger one. "I really am glad you're here, Nance. It's been too long."

"It has," I agreed. "We'll start making up for lost time tonight. And what better place to do it than here?" I glanced out one of the large picture windows, where the last of the day's dim light was fading. The time for the gala was fast approaching—and from the look of it, it promised to be a legendary night!

~

CHAPTER TWO

A Night
on Mount
Olympus

PUTTING ON MY COSTUME THAT NIGHT
felt less like getting ready for a party than getting ready
for a war. After donning my cream-colored tunic and
flowing skirt, I strapped on a pair of black gladiator
sandals, fastened leather cuffs around each wrist, and
added a shiny brass breastplate that I'd picked up at a
costume shop in River Heights. Finally, after tying my
hair up in a bun, I set a red-crested brass helmet on my
head and secured it with the chin strap.

When I was all done, I snatched up the shield and spear props that I'd brought and took a look in the full-length mirror on the back of the bedroom door. I couldn't help but smile at my reflection. "Not bad, Drew," I muttered to myself, turning this way and that. "Not bad at all!" Even Athena herself would have been proud.

A moment later there was a knock at the door. "Enter!" I said theatrically. The door swung open, and on the other side stood two characters straight out of Mount Olympus. "Bess!" I exclaimed. "George! You both look amazing!"

"Oh, thank you, *darling*," Bess said, gliding into the room. She wore an off-the-shoulder gown of filmy aquamarine fabric that gathered around her feet like an ocean wave crashing. Tiny, multicolored seashells were stitched in a swirling pattern down the side of the dress. Her blond hair, which was usually shoulder length, was now so long that it cascaded halfway down her back in wavy curls. *Extensions*, I thought. *No wonder it took her so long to get ready!* "So," she asked, blinking her long, mascara-laden eyelashes at me, "do I look like Aphrodite?"

I shook my head in wonder. "I think if you looked up Aphrodite on the Internet, it would come up with a picture of you," I answered. It was a no-brainer that starry-eyed Bess would choose the goddess of love for her costume.

I turned to George and grinned. "So *that's* why you had all those feathers stuck to your bag!"

"Well, I sure wasn't kidnapping pigeons, if that's what you thought." George chuckled, and then executed a sharp bow. "Hermes, messenger of the gods—at your service, my lady." She was wearing a white silk camisole over a pair of gold-sequined shorts. Strappy gold sandals, with tiny white wings affixed to them, adorned her feet, and she wore a winged gold bike helmet over her short hair. An application of gold eye shadow and blush completed her look. She saw my gaze linger on her face and rolled her eyes. "Bess insisted on the makeup," she said.

"Oh, stop whining," Bess said. "You know it looks good."

George shrugged, grinning, and turned her attention back to me. "Well!" she said. "At least we know no one's going to mess with us tonight! Not with Nancy 'Warrior Princess' Drew at our side!"

"I had a feeling you'd go with Athena," Bess said, studying my costume with approval. "What with her being the goddess of wisdom and all."

"Wisdom, courage, law, justice, war strategy, mathematics," I listed.

"All right, all right." George held her hands up in surrender. "Athena's awesome, okay? But come on, who do you really want to hang out at a party with? The goddess of law? Or the god of literature and poetry and sports and wit?"

I crossed my arms and gave George a hard look. "Are you saying you're cooler than me?"

George hesitated. "Not with that spear in your hand, I'm not."

We all laughed, and after a few last-minute makeup and costume tweaks, we left the room. The party was almost ready to begin!

We walked into the main entry hall to find Iris greeting guests as they came in the door, all of them shaking out umbrellas and peeling off raincoats. She was wearing an explosively colorful costume—a long, layered gown made up of red, yellow, green, blue, and purple satin that seemed to shine with inner light. On her back was a pair of huge, iridescent fairy wings.

"Wow!" I exclaimed when she turned to greet me. "Your costume . . . it's absolutely breathtaking. Who are you dressed as?"

"Iris, of course!" Iris laughed. "My namesake. Goddess of the rainbow!"

While Iris and Bess oohed and aahed over each other's outfits, George and I made our way into the ballroom, which was already humming with the sounds of conversation, laughter, and prerecorded bouzouki music. A long buffet table boasted platters of stuffed grape leaves, bite-size spinach-and-feta-cheese pies, and triangles of pita bread served with Greek caviar. But before we could reach the table, a server in a purple-belted toga glided over to us. He was carrying a tray of glasses filled to the brim with an amber-colored liquid. "What's this?" I asked him.

"The nectar of the gods," the young man said with a smile.

"Can you be a little more specific?" George asked.

"Local apple cider simmered with honey, cinnamon, orange peel, and butter."

"*Butter?*" George exclaimed. "Oh, I'll have one, please." She picked up a glass and took a long swig. "Mmm," she moaned, licking her lips. "Now *that* is good. Only the gods would think to put butter in a drink!"

I took a glass myself and had a taste of the sweet, cool, and velvety mixture. "Delicious," I agreed. "Speaking of gods—look at all these people!"

George and I took a moment to really gaze around the room at the other guests. We weren't the only ones to go all out with our costumes! I saw Medusa, half a dozen rubber snakes slithering on her head; a frightening, black-robed Hades with his hair and beard dyed a fiery orange; and Demeter, a woman with hair the color of wheat, dancing in a grass-green dress covered in silk flowers. "It's like a dream," I murmured, and George nodded.

"Nancy!" I turned to see Iris waving me over from across the room. She and Bess were standing with two men—one only a little older than me, and the other a handsome, thirtysomething gentleman with auburn hair. The younger man was dressed in a simple, rust-colored tunic, with two enormous white feathered wings stretching out from his back. *He must be Icarus,* I thought, remembering the story of the winged boy who flew too close to the sun. The gentleman next to him shone under the overhead lights, for his costume was made almost entirely of golden fabric. The headdress he wore sported wavy gold spires all around it, making his head look like the center of a tiny sun. George and I made our way over to them through the crowd. "There you are, ladies," Iris said as we approached. "I'd like you both to meet two very special people! This is Sebastian Rivera, the classics department's star student"—she gestured to the younger man, who blushed at the compliment—"and Dr. Fletcher Brown, one of our esteemed classics faculty." The other man beamed and took my hand in his.

"Athena, I presume," he said, his voice rich and sonorous. "Charmed."

"Let me guess," I said. "Apollo, god of sun and light?"

"Ah, I see Iris was correct," Dr. Brown said with a smile. "Miss Nancy Drew is indeed a master of deduction!"

"Well, I wouldn't go that far," I demurred. "It's quite an impressive costume. I'm sure most of the guests could figure out who you are."

"You give them too much credit, my dear," Dr. Brown replied. "And who is your trickster friend here?"

"George Fayne—pleasure to meet you, sir!" George pumped the man's hand. "I promise your wallet is safe from me tonight," she joked.

"A likely story, coming from the patron god of thieves!" Dr. Brown said, his eyebrow raised in amusement.

"Sebastian," Bess was saying to the younger man. "I have to say, those wings of yours are amazing! Where did you get them?"

Sebastian looked at Bess and grinned shyly, his light brown skin reddening once again. "Call me Bash," he replied, brushing a lock of curly black hair out of his eyes. "And actually, I made them."

George's eyes bugged. "What?" she exclaimed. "Whew! And I thought it took a long time to make these little guys!" She gestured to the wings on each side of her helmet. "Yours must have taken an eternity!"

"Pretty much," Bash agreed. "I think I still have superglue on my fingers. So much superglue . . ." He shook his head.

"If only the real Icarus had the luxury of superglue, he would have lived to tell the tale!" Dr. Brown said. He smiled—a dazzling, open smile—and the rest of us couldn't help but join him.

Bess leaned over to whisper in my ear. "If he were my professor, I don't think I'd be able to concentrate in class at all!"

I rolled my eyes. "Bess, I think you're taking this 'goddess of love' thing a little too seriously. Cupid's arrow is meant for other people—not you!"

"Oho!" A familiar voice split through the low hum of conversation, as Dr. Pappas came toward us, the crowd parting before him. He wore a flowing, off-white tunic and a laurel wreath on his head, and held a silver walking stick in the shape of a lightning bolt. "What did I tell you about having too much fun without me?"

"My lord Zeus!" Dr. Brown exclaimed, opening his arms wide. "How you honor us with your presence."

Dr. Pappas clapped the professor on the shoulder and chuckled. "Flattery will get you nowhere, my dear man. I see you've met my daughter's young friends? You all look magnificent tonight! I hope the three of you are considering Oracle College after graduation"—Dr. Pappas winked conspiratorially—"because this institution is about to be truly put on the map! Ambitious professors like Fletcher here are on the brink of making it big. Aren't you, son?"

Dr. Brown feigned exasperation, blowing out his cheeks. "First it's burnt offerings you want, and now this? Papa George, you are one tough customer."

Dr. Pappas laughed. "Don't be modest, Fletcher. You make Oracle proud. Now, I must go and greet the rest of my subjects!" With that, Dr. Pappas dived back into the crowd, roaring with mirth as he caught sight of another group of costumed colleagues.

We all watched him go, Iris shaking her head with amusement.

"Your father certainly makes his expectations known," Dr. Brown said. "After that speech, I think I need a drink! It was a pleasure meeting you, ladies."

Once Dr. Brown went off in search of the bar, Bess and George began chatting with Bash about college life. Before I could get wrapped up in that conversation, Iris pulled me away to point out some other notable guests at the gala.

After an hour or so of chitchat with Iris's friends and professors, the gala was in full swing. A six-piece band had replaced the prerecorded music, and the crowd of dancers was virtually impenetrable. In an attempt to reach the buffet table, we skirted the outer edges of the ballroom, and I noticed a middle-aged woman standing alone near one of the picture windows. She was gazing silently outside at the storm, her expression thoughtful. Unlike so many of the other guests, this woman's costume was understated, elegant. She wore a long, midnight-blue gown with a scooped neck; a wooden bow and a quiver full of arrows were slung across her back. The long gray-white braids that cascaded down her back glowed ethereally in the dim light, their paleness in stark contrast with the blue of her dress and the deep brown of her skin.

I stopped and whispered to Iris, "Who is that?"

Iris turned to see the woman and whispered back, "Oh! That's Dr. Stone. She's a classics professor, too— like Dr. Brown. She's been here *forever*. Even longer than Dad, I think. She's brilliant, apparently, but not very popular. She's a tough grader, and students fail her classes constantly because their work isn't up to her standards. Honestly, most people are terrified of her."

I grimaced. "Is she that bad?"

Iris shrugged. "I wouldn't know for certain—I'm only repeating what I've heard other people say. Apparently, she also keeps this talking parrot in her office as a pet," she confided. "Dad says it's against regulations, but because it's her, he doesn't say anything. He said she loves that bird like her own kid." We both stood for a moment, watching Dr. Stone take a small sip from her glass of nectar. "She wears that same costume every year, you know," Iris added. "Artemis, goddess of the hunt. It's a great dress, but why not mix it up a little?"

"Maybe Artemis means something special to her," I guessed.

"Maybe. Hey, look!" Iris's eyes lit up as she caught sight of half a dozen servers parading into the room with trays. "Desserts! Oh, Nancy, you simply *have* to try these little baklavas. It's pastry and nuts and honey and—"

"Yeah, I'm coming," I said, my eyes still on Dr. Stone. There was something about the woman that piqued my interest. *What's her story?* I wondered. As I watched, the woman leaned forward and gripped the windowsill in front of her. She closed her eyes, her mouth pressed into a tight line as if in pain.

I darted forward, laying my hand gently on her shoulder. "Excuse me, ma'am," I said. "Are you all right?"

Dr. Stone spun around, surprised at my touch. She blinked at me, her eyes unfocused for a moment before she regained her bearings. "Yes, yes, I'm fine," she replied, standing up straight. She glanced at the silver watch on her wrist and then back up at me. "Excuse me," she said brusquely, and without another word, she brushed past me and toward the stairs up to the balcony level.

Maybe she ate a bad olive, I thought as I made my way toward Iris, who was busy piling a plate with Greek pastries. *Or maybe she just really doesn't like parties.* I could understand that. Events like this could be overwhelming for some—the noise, the crush of the crowd, the forced small talk. Even I was starting to crave a little solitude and fresh air right about now.

Maybe Dr. Stone just needed a minute to herself. I craned my head to scan the balcony level and caught a glimpse of Dr. Stone accepting a drink from a server up there and taking a seat on one of the chaise lounges. There were some other guests mingling near the railing, and I saw Bash, the boy I'd met earlier, stop and talk with Dr. Stone. I turned back to the party in front of me, trying to see what had become of Iris and her quest for pastries.

A few minutes later the dance music came to an end, and Dr. Pappas's voice came over a speaker system. "May I have your attention, please!" he said.

The crowd quieted immediately, and every eye turned toward Dr. Pappas, who was standing on the part of the balcony that jutted out about eight feet into the ballroom, surrounded on three sides by clay-colored metal railings. The guests gathered on the dance floor beneath him and gazed up at their beaming host. "My friends!" Dr. Pappas said into a microphone. "Thank you for joining me at the fifth annual Greek Gala!" The crowd erupted in cheers, many raising half-full glasses of nectar and red wine into the air. "I am so pleased to see each of your smiling faces tonight—especially you, Dr. Hall. It wouldn't be a party without you!" Dr. Pappas gestured to a short, older man dressed as Dionysus, his purple toga dripping with bunches of wax grapes. "Dr. Hall takes the job of 'god of drinking and ritual madness' very, very seriously!" Everyone laughed.

Outside, the storm continued to rage, and after a particularly loud clap of thunder, the overhead lights flickered. "Well, well," Dr. Pappas said after a collective gasp from the guests. "It seems the gods do not approve of my jokes. So I will get to the point! As you all know, every year, a special member of the Oracle community is chosen to deliver a speech, and tonight, I am honored to introduce—"

At that moment, an event planner tapped Dr. Pappas on the shoulder. The college president stopped mid-sentence, covering the microphone with one hand. The event planner whispered something into Dr. Pappas's ear, and a look of concern crossed the man's face. As he turned back to the microphone, he cleared his throat and smiled once again. "Excuse the interruption," he said. "As I was saying, I am honored to introduce one of Oracle's finest students, a young man taking our renowned classics department by storm. In his three years at our institution, he has brought revolutionary ideas into the classroom and has been instrumental in revitalizing the Eta Sigma Phi Honor Society for classical studies. Ladies and gentlemen, I give you Mr. Sebastian Rivera!"

The crowd erupted in applause as Bash, living up to his nickname, bashfully approached the microphone. His huge white wings stretched out behind him and caught the light, making him look angelic as he looked down on the assembled guests. When the room fell silent, Bash took a deep breath and spoke. "Thank you, President Pappas, for your kind words. And thank you for believing in me, and awarding me with the Delphi Scholarship. Without that funding, made possible by people like you all"—here, Bash gestured at the crowd— "I wouldn't have been able to attend Oracle and follow my dreams as I have since I came here."

"Oh, he's good," Iris muttered in my ear. "Buttering up the donors, too!"

"I have so many people to thank for all the opportunities I've been given in these past few years," Bash continued. "But there is one person in particular I want to highlight tonight. Someone who has opened up my mind to new possibilities, inspired me with new ideas, and constantly challenged me to push myself toward new heights, never accepting less than my best."

A murmur drifted through the crowd as people looked around, trying to find the person Bash was talking about. I caught sight of Dr. Brown standing nearby, looking up at Bash. The people standing nearby were pointing at Dr. Brown and whispering to one another. *I suppose Bash is talking about him*, I thought. *After all, Iris did say he's the most popular professor in the department.*

"Without this person's constant support," Bash was saying, "I would never have achieved the things I have here at Oracle. Please, can everyone give a big round of applause to—" He stepped toward the front

~ 34 ~

of the balcony and gripped the railing in front of him, craning his head to scan the crowd.

Another thunderclap boomed overhead, causing the house to tremble around us. Again, the lights began to flicker, throwing the ballroom into intermittent darkness.

Because of the flickering lights, the next few moments seemed to happen in slow motion. One second, Bash was leaning forward on the balcony railing, and the next second, the railing was emitting an earsplitting whine as it fell free of the walls around it and toppled to the ballroom floor.

Right behind it, in a flurry of white wings and rippling red cloth, Bash was falling too.

The room erupted in screams and shattering glass, and then the lights went out for good.

CHAPTER THREE

The Fall of Icarus

IN THE DARKNESS, THERE WAS PANIC.

I struggled to keep my footing as bodies pushed past me from all sides, with some guests blindly rushing away from the place where the balcony came down, streaming toward the only illumination left in the room—a glowing exit sign. Others were using their cell phones as flashlights, panning around the room and shouting for people to stay where they were. No one quite knew what had happened—only that there was danger and that they wanted to get away from it.

I commanded my mind to be calm, pulled my own

phone from my purse, and switched on the flashlight feature. Its narrow beam of white light pierced the gloom, highlighting flashes of frightened faces and reflecting off glass shards littering the floor. I slowly made my way forward, against the current of people flowing out of the room.

Finally I saw him.

Bash was lying facedown on top of the balcony railing, his great white wings splayed out around him, bent and broken. Several other guests stood by, their faces pale with shock as I shone my light across the scene. "Oh no, no, no," a young woman in a nymph costume moaned as she stared at Bash's still form. "Is he—?"

Swallowing back the wave of dread that rose from the pit of my stomach, I knelt at Bash's side and touched the side of his neck. To my relief, I felt a pulse fluttering against my fingertips. "He's alive," I said, my voice shaky. "But he needs help—now. Has anyone called 911?"

"Yes—yes, they're on their way now," a man replied.

As if on cue, the cry of an ambulance cut through the hum of noise in the ballroom, getting louder by the second. At the same moment, catering staff carrying electric lanterns streamed into the room, filling the space with an eerie sort of light and throwing long shadows against the walls. Within minutes, the crowd was parting to accommodate the paramedics, their uniforms glossy with rain as they ran toward Bash.

The room was hushed as the paramedics removed the wings from Bash's back and gently loaded him onto a gurney. Almost as quickly as they came, the men were gone. I listened as the siren began blaring once more, the sound soon swallowed by the storm as the ambulance rushed to the hospital. What would happen to Bash? I wondered. Would he be all right?

Moments later, the lights in the ballroom flickered to life—I shielded my eyes from the sudden glare. Someone must have finally gotten to the circuit breakers and gotten the power back on. Guests began wandering more freely about the room, getting their bearings.

"There you are."

I felt a hand on my shoulder, and it snapped me out of my reverie. "Bess," I said, turning to see her worried face. "Oh, it was so awful."

Bess nodded. "I'm amazed that no one else got hurt!" she said. "Luckily, there was no one standing directly underneath the balcony, so the railing just fell on the floor. Poor Bash. What a terrible accident."

"Yes," I agreed, touching my head. Suddenly something felt very, very wrong. I realized that I had a pounding headache. It almost felt like something was inside my brain, trying to punch its way out. *This must be how Zeus felt when Athena was about to burst out of his head*, I thought,. "I think I need to sit down," I said to Bess, and lurched toward the nearest table.

Bess took my arm and led me to a chair. She caught sight of George coming our way and told her to bring me some water. When George came back with a pitcher and some empty glasses, we all sat together, drinking and talking about what had happened. All around us, groups of people stood together, murmuring quietly to one another, while caterers swept through the room trying to clean up the mess. Clearly, the party wasn't going to recover from this. I noticed a girl sitting across the table from us, staring at the place where Bash had fallen, tears streaming down her face. She had glossy, dark brown hair, and amber skin perfectly complemented by her forest-green Persephone costume. Bess and George followed my gaze and fell quiet when they saw her too.

"Are you all right?" I asked the girl.

"Oh!" she said, startled to find us looking at her. She quickly snatched up a clean napkin from the table and dabbed at her eyes. "Yeah, I'm okay."

"Was Bash a friend of yours?" I asked.

The girl nodded. "Actually, he and I are dating. It's only been a month, but it was going so well. I wanted to go in the ambulance with him, but they told me I should stay here. I'm just so . . ." Her face crumpled, and her shoulders shook with sobs.

George quickly poured the girl a glass of water and pushed it into her hands. She took a shaky sip and mouthed *Thank you* at us, as if she didn't trust herself to speak again without crying.

"I bet he's going to be just fine," Bess said, smiling reassuringly. "He'll be up on his feet again in no time, you'll see."

"I hope you're right," the girl murmured.

Just then a young man emerged from the crowd, his eyes scanning the room until they landed on us. He was tall with broad shoulders and wore a gray chest plate and cuffs clearly meant to be an Ares costume. He made his way over to our table and touched the girl on the shoulder. "Daniela," he said. "Let me take you home."

When Daniela saw who it was, her expression hardened. "I'm waiting to get a ride to the hospital, Mason," she said without meeting his eyes.

"Let me take you," he insisted.

Daniela shook her head.

"Don't be that way," he pleaded. "I'm just trying to help."

Daniela snatched up her handbag from the table

and stood. "I don't need your help, okay?" And with that, she strode off, disappearing into the crowd.

Mason watched her go. He must have felt our eyes on him, because a moment later he turned to us and gave an awkward smile. "She's just upset," he said with a shrug. "Crazy thing, what happened to Bash. Him dressed as Icarus and all—it's kind of funny." When Mason saw the looks on our faces, he stammered to elaborate. "Uh, not funny ha-ha, of course—I mean funny like, weird."

"Was Bash a friend of yours?" I asked.

"Oh, everyone loves Bash. For being such a shy little dude, he somehow manages to be the most popular guy in the department." Mason stared at the place where Bash had lain just moments ago and bit his lip. "Anyway, I'd better go see if Daniela's okay. Nice talking to you."

After he'd gone, George let out a long breath, her eyebrows raised. "Boy," she said. "Some guys just can't take a hint, can they?"

"No," I said, thoughtful. "And did you notice? He never answered my question."

The crackle of a microphone coming on interrupted my thoughts. I stood to see Dr. Pappas standing on the stage where the band had been playing, his face shiny with sweat. He looked like he'd aged ten years in the last thirty minutes. "Excuse me," he said into the microphone, his voice husky with emotion. "Please, may I have your attention? In light of this terrible accident, I'm afraid we must cut the gala short. Thank you for coming, and I assure you that I'll let the Oracle community know of any news about Sebastian as soon as I have it."

The assembled guests immediately began gathering their things and making for the exit. My headache had subsided—though I still felt wrong somehow—so I told Bess and George that I was going to try and find Iris. Weaving through the crowd, I bumped shoulders with Dr. Brown, who apologized as I stumbled.

"So sorry—oh, hello. Nancy, was it?" he said. He tried to smile, but it didn't reach his eyes.

"Yes," I said. "Are you all right? You're awfully pale."

Dr. Brown nodded. "I'll be fine, thank you. It's just that . . . that boy was so bright, he had so much potential—"

I laid a gentle hand on Dr. Brown's arm. "He still does," I said. "We don't know the extent of his injuries yet. He may come out of this as good as new."

Dr. Brown sniffed and brought his hand to his mouth. "I do hope you're right. Good night, Nancy."

By now, most of the guests had gone, so it wasn't difficult to see Iris towering over the remaining catering staff as she helped them remove the uneaten food from the buffet table. "Iris," I said as I approached her. "I'm so sorry about the gala. I know you put a lot of work into it."

Iris shook her head vigorously, dabbing at her eyes with a tissue. "Oh, pooh on the party. All that matters is that Sebastian comes out of this okay. I just can't imagine how this could have happened. That balcony railing had just been replaced a couple of years ago—it was virtually brand-new! How it simply fell away with the smallest amount of pressure, I'll never know." Just then George and Bess came up, also giving Iris their condolences about the accident. She thanked them, sniffed, and pulled her shoulders back. "Well, that's enough blubbering for one day! Time to pull myself together—there's still work to be done. You girls go ahead and turn in for the night. I'll see you all in the morning."

I gave Iris a hug, and we all bade her a good night. After the girls and I went our separate ways upstairs, I let myself into my bedroom, pulled the heavy helmet from my head, and tossed my spear and shield on the dresser. It was a relief to unburden myself from all those heavy things, but I still felt weighed down somehow. *Maybe a nice, hot shower before bed will do the trick,* I thought. Pulling off my sandals, I tossed them next to the still-sodden sneakers that I had worn that afternoon when we'd arrived. The sole of one overturned shoe was still encrusted with those small, clay-colored fragments I'd stepped on while Iris was giving me the tour of the house. I brushed them off into the wastebasket and was once again struck with the oddness of that pile of flakes sitting right in the middle of the floor in the ballroom. Suddenly a thought struck me, and that sick sensation I'd been feeling ever since the accident intensified.

Without another thought, I bolted out of the room, barefoot, and ran back downstairs, passing Iris as I went. "Nancy!" she said, startled. "What—?"

But I couldn't stop now, not until I found out if my suspicions were true.

The ballroom was virtually empty now; only a lone staff member was left sweeping the floor. The fallen balcony railing was leaning against the wall, and a dusty mess of plaster and other detritus was scattered across the dance floor. "Miss," the staff member said. "Can I help you?"

"No, thank you," I replied. "Hey, listen. You've had a long day and you must be exhausted. Why don't you call it a night and I'll finish up here for you? I'm feeling a little restless and wouldn't mind a little work before bed."

The man looked at me strangely but nodded and smiled. "As you wish, miss. Thank you."

I stood on the exact spot on the floor where I'd remembered stepping into the fragments and looked up. Just as I'd thought, I found myself staring directly up at one edge of the balcony. Since it jutted out farther into the room than any of the other clay-colored metal railings lining the second story, there was no question that the fragments had come from the exact same railing that had fallen.

"There you are!" Iris exclaimed as she came into the room. "Nancy, what in the world is going on? You come tearing down the stairs like a woman possessed, barefoot and crazy-eyed—"

"Iris," I said, my voice serious. "This wasn't an accident."

Iris gaped at me. "What?" she said.

"Someone did this on purpose," I said.

Iris gave me a skeptical look. "Nancy, I know mystery is sort of your *thing*, but I think in this case you're going a little overboard. It *was* an accident!"

"No, Iris—I'm serious!" I replied, pulling her back as she started to shuffle sleepily away. "Please, just listen.

Do you remember that stuff I stepped on earlier today? It's the same stuff on the floor right now." I pointed at the clay-colored dust that littered the floor. "It's paint from the balcony railing. It has to be—there's nothing else in this room that matches that color exactly. And the pile of fragments was here"—I gestured above us to the now-broken balcony—"right under where Bash was standing for the speech."

Iris crossed her arms. "Okay . . . there was some paint on the ground. So what?"

"*So* that means that someone was tampering with the balcony *right before* the party started. You told me that the catering staff had already been in early that morning to clean the room, so it must have happened sometime after that. They must have used a screw-driver to loosen the bolts that secured the railing to the wall, the paint would have peeled away in the process and fell to the floor below. They left it tight enough to stay attached, but loose enough to give way if anyone leaned on it. Which is exactly what Bash did during his speech."

Iris still didn't look convinced.

I walked over to where the fallen railing was leaning and knelt down to inspect the sides. "You see?" I said, pointing to the holes. "The paint is stripped. But only from the holes that would have been securing the railing to the supporting beams on each side. This was done in a hurry and with a screwdriver—a professional with a drill wouldn't have done this kind of damage. It's sabotage, Iris."

Iris stared at the holes for a moment before staggering back, her eyes wide. "Are you sure?" she asked.

"I'm positive."

"But who would do such a thing? And why?"

I took a deep breath and let it out slowly. That sick feeling had fallen away and been replaced by a kind of electric tingling that I had become very familiar with over the years. "I don't know," I said. "But I'm going to find out."

CHAPTER FOUR

~∾~

A Jealous God

A NEW DAY DAWNED BRIGHT AND CLEAR—
but my mind remained clouded with questions.

After a sleepless night, I rose from bed and
parted the curtains to see the buildings of Oracle
still sparkling with rain from the storm. I pushed
away the wave of fatigue and focused on the day
ahead. The girls and I had planned on returning to
River Heights this morning, but I had already told
Iris that I'd be sticking around to investigate Bash's
so-called "accident." I threw on some clothes and
went out to find Bess and George—they still didn't

~ 50 ~

know about the little discovery I'd made the night before.

In the hallway I ran into Bess, who was dressed impeccably as usual. She wore a flowy, sage-colored skirt and a lacy sleeveless blouse, her blond hair pulled into an updo that was probably done carelessly but managed to look flawless. "Oh, Bess," I said with a sigh. "You look as fresh as a daisy. Could I borrow a little of your energy, please?"

Bess looked at me with concern. "Wow, you didn't get much sleep, did you, Nance? You look positively worn out!"

"I am," I agreed. "But that's not important now. I need to talk to you and George right away. Something's come up, and I've got to stay here at Oracle for at least another day."

Bess gave me a sidelong look. "Let me guess—is there a mystery afoot?"

I nodded. "Of mythic proportions."

We found George still in her bedroom—still in her bed. "Mungggh," she groaned as Bess threw open the curtains and flooded the room with sunlight. "Why . . . ," George moaned. "What have I done to deserve this?"

"Rise and shine, Hermes," Bess sang. "Nancy's on the case."

George sat up and stared at us, bleary-eyed. Her short dark hair was pressed into a cowlick that made her head look like a skateboard ramp. "What time is it?" she asked.

I glanced at my watch. "Eight thirty."

George covered her face with her hands and fell back onto the pillows. "No mysteries before nine a.m.!" she bellowed.

After listening to some more grumbling, we got a doughnut and a cup of coffee into George, and she managed to throw on a pair of jeans and a T-shirt and join the world of the living. The three of us gathered in the sitting area of the bedroom, and I brought the others up to speed about the events of the night before.

"Sabotage, eh?" George mused. "Well, that certainly

would explain why the balcony came right off like it did. But Bash seemed like such a stand-up guy—who would want to hurt someone like him?"

"Even saints have enemies," I said. "We just need to find out who they are."

Bess bit her lip. "Yeah . . . about that 'we' part," she began.

George cleared her throat. "Right," she added. "You see, Nancy—"

"I just can't stay," Bess blurted. "As much as I'd love to help with the case, I have to get back to River Heights today. I promised my mom I'd help with the yard sale—"

"And I already told my grandpa I'd come and fix his computer this afternoon," George broke in. "And delete a bunch of junk e-mails. And update his malware. And install his new printer. And—" She blew out her cheeks. "Anyway, it's a full day's work, and I don't want to let him down."

I felt my shoulders slump. How was I going to solve this mystery without my two best friends? Bess and

George must have seen the look on my face, because they both rushed to apologize.

"We're so sorry, Nancy!" Bess said. "I would stay if I could, but—"

"No, no," I interrupted, waving her apology away. "Don't be silly!"

"You can call us anytime," George said. "You know my phone is practically glued to my hand as it is!"

"Yeah, of course," I reassured them. "It will be fine—really." I tried to sound casual, but neither of the girls looked convinced.

A knock at the door interrupted the moment. "Come in!" George called out.

Iris burst through the door in a flurry of yellow ruffles and polka dots, the brightness of her dress equal to the sunny smile on her face. "Hello and good morning, my dear friends!" she sang.

After my revelation last night, I was surprised to see Iris looking so happy. But then I remembered that time when we were eight years old and her parakeet died. At first she cried, but later that day she'd invited all the neighborhood kids over to participate in a bird-themed celebration to pay tribute to her late pet. She played host the entire time, laughing and smiling as everyone made bird masks out of paper plates and construction paper. I guess putting on a happy face was just the way Iris coped with hardship.

"What's going on, Iris?" I asked. "Have you heard anything from the hospital about Bash?"

"As a matter of fact, I have! Good news—Bash is going to be okay!"

I got to my feet—this *was* good news.

"Oh! How wonderful," Bess said.

"Is he awake?" I asked urgently. After all, Bash would know better than anyone else who might want to hurt him.

Iris's smile faltered. "Well, no, not yet," she admitted. "He's still unconscious. But they say he's stable. There's just no telling exactly when he'll wake up, unfortunately."

I sighed. For now, my investigation would have to

continue without Bash's help. And without George and Bess's help either.

I felt about as sunny as a storm cloud.

Iris glanced my way and must have noticed the look on my face. "Buck up, Sherlock!" she said, giving me a friendly punch to the shoulder. "Negative Nancys don't solve mysteries!"

Bess and George laughed—but a moment later George sat up like she'd just been struck by lightning. "That's it!" she exclaimed. "You don't need us, Nancy— you've got Iris! She'll be your wing-girl for this caper. Won't you, Iris?"

My heart lifted a little, a bit of light peeking through the clouds.

Iris looked back and forth between us, and then put her hands on her hips. "Well, I'm still going to have to go to class here and there—but of course I will!" she finally said. "I'm sure I can squeeze a little private investigation into my schedule. But I *have* to see if I've got any detective wear in my wardrobe. A girl can't solve a crime in just any old thing!"

And just like that, Iris cleared out my dreary mood like a fierce wind blowing away the clouds. "Oh, Iris," I said, giving her hand a squeeze. "I'm so glad."

"Sure you are!" she replied. "Now, what do you think . . . a brown tweed pantsuit? Or is that too on-the-nose?"

Later that morning, after I'd seen George and Bess off in a bus back to River Heights, Iris and I were walking down a path from the president's mansion to the campus quad. Maple trees on either side of us created a canopy above us, their fiery orange leaves heralding the coming season. All the world was perfumed with the smoky, crisp scent of autumn. I took a deep breath, hoping the fresh air would give my tired brain the jolt of energy it needed to start thinking about the case.

"You want to pick up some coffee at the campus café?" Iris asked.

"You read my mind," I replied.

A few minutes later we'd arrived in the center of campus, which was crowded with students and professors heading to their morning classes. A squat, cylindrical building stood in the middle of it all, with the redbrick academic buildings radiating out from it like spokes on a wheel. Iris led me inside the central building, the Commons, which housed administrative offices, the campus store, and an eatery. The café stood under a sign picturing a cartoon Sphinx holding a mug of coffee.

"Drinx?" I read with a smirk.

"Yeah," Iris said with a groan. "It was Dad's idea. He's got the cheesiest sense of humor. It would be embarrassing if it wasn't so adorable."

We each bought a large coffee and found an empty table. After a few rejuvenating sips, I set down my cup and said, "Okay, let's get down to business. I need to know more about Bash to figure out who would want to hurt him. With Bash out of the way, would that leave an opening for another student to be the star of the department? Do you know of anyone who might be jealous of his success?"

Iris tapped her chin with one manicured finger. "I

suppose someone could be jealous of Bash, but there isn't anyone who springs to mind. He's a shy, sweet guy. Not exactly a show-off who rubs people the wrong way."

I bit my lip. "Okay, maybe we're just looking at a prank gone wrong?" I guessed. "I mean, I've heard of all kinds of awful pranks happening on college campuses—maybe this could have been one of those? Someone could have wanted Bash to fall but didn't realize how much it would hurt him to hit the ground from that height." Then a thought occurred to me. "Actually, if they knew he was going to be wearing the Icarus costume, maybe they thought it would be funny to replicate the events from the myth itself— the fall of Icarus."

Iris took a sip of coffee. "It's possible," she said. "Though not the norm here at Oracle. But you never know—students here *are* very competitive. If you want to sniff around, you could start by going to the coed dorms at the top of the hill—that's where Bash lives. His girlfriend, too, I think. She might be able to give you some insight." Iris glanced at the clock on her phone and gasped. "Shoot, I'm going to be late for class! I've got to run. But it's a good time for you to do some snooping around—text me after and let me know if you find anything. We'll meet up in the afternoon once my classes are done."

I nodded. "Just keep your eyes and ears open—you never know what you might overhear. Sometimes insignificant details can turn out to be crucial clues later on." I bit back more instructions—I didn't want to sound as if I was lecturing her like one of her professors.

"Yes, Detective Drew," Iris said, saluting, her mouth pressed into a hard line. "Whatever you say, boss!"

I rolled my eyes and laughed. I guess I needn't have worried. "Don't let me down, kid," I said in a mock-serious tone. "I'm counting on you."

Iris chuckled and patted my hand. "Seriously, though, I'm your girl, Nance! If there's a clue to be found, I'll sniff it out."

Bash's dormitory was an ivy-covered redbrick building that sat atop a steep hill, its square middle section bookended by two conical towers. Doing my best to look casual and blend in, I waited until one of the residents used his keycard to open the security door and snuck in behind him.

Inside, the hallway was virtually empty—Iris had said that a lot of students would be in their morning classes. The white walls were plastered with colorful flyers advertising upcoming campus events and parties, and many of the apartment doors were decorated with all manner of funny drawings and messages to roommates. Unfortunately, there weren't any names on the doors. How was I going to find Bash's room?

My question was answered a few minutes later, after I'd climbed the stairs to the second floor and spied a small shrine erected outside one of the doors. Small bouquets of flowers littered the ground, and the door itself was a riot of different-colored sticky notes, each of them sending well-wishes to the occupant of the room. Which, of course, was Bash.

Well, I thought. *Problem solved.* I listened at the door for any sound—after all, for all I knew, Bash had a roommate. But there was only silence. Pulling a credit card from my wallet, I checked both ends of the hallway for witnesses and jimmied the lock. Within a minute of finding the room, I was inside.

The room within was small and neat, with a desk facing the window and a twin bed pushed into the corner. *Whew,* I thought, *it looks like a single. No roommate to worry about.* I stepped over a pile of white feathers and a glue gun—evidence of Bash's late-night wing construction—and went to the desk. Bash's silver laptop sat half-covered in marked-up term papers. Upon closer examination, I discovered that many of the papers were for an ancient philosophy course taught by Dr. Stone. "You can do better," read one note in purple ink, followed by a large letter *B*. Considering Bash was the department's star student, I found the grade surprising. *Iris was right,* I thought. *Dr. Stone really is a tough customer.*

I brushed the papers aside and opened up the laptop. I know, I know—usually it's a big no-no to break into someone's place and snoop around their computer.

But I always tell myself that in the pursuit of justice, some rules just have to be broken.

The desktop blinked on right away, and I began clicking through Bash's file folders, looking for anything that could be a clue. Curious, I sorted the files by date created, and opened up the most recent one, dated yesterday evening. It was a document full of notes from Dr. Stone's class. *This must have happened right before the gala!* Unfortunately, it didn't prove to be very helpful. Just three pages of lecture notes, followed by a quick rundown of a group assignment due in two weeks. Bash had written down the names of the people in his group—Maria, Gwendolyn, Eleanor, and Mason—and their topic, which was about justice in Plato's *Republic*. Frustrated, I closed the laptop and scanned the room again. After five more minutes of searching, I was still empty-handed. Then I heard the murmur of voices outside the door. First very low, and then louder and louder. Checking the time on my phone, I realized about an hour had passed since I'd left Iris at the café. The morning class period must be over, and some students were returning to the dorm! I had to get out of there, fast, before I got caught.

Returning the room to the state that I'd found it, I slipped out into the hallway and was on my way back down the stairs when I heard voices from the landing below. They sounded so familiar that I peered down the stairwell to see who it was. Sure enough, there were Daniela and the boy from the gala. *Looks like he still hasn't given up,* I thought. Though they were speaking in low voices, the stairwell acted like an echo chamber, and I was able to hear them clearly from my perch up above.

"For the last time," Daniela was saying, "I'm with Bash now, okay?"

"But Bash might be in the hospital for weeks! Months!" Mason argued. "What are you going to do?"

Daniela huffed. "Oh, I don't know—*live my life?* Contrary to what you might think, I can take care of myself, thank you very much. However long it takes, I'll wait."

"But baby, I miss you."

"It's over, Mason. I'm not your 'baby' anymore."

There was a pause. "You're making a mistake," Mason growled.

"No," Daniela answered. "My mistake was ever dating you in the first place."

I saw Mason turn away and throw open the stairwell door, slamming it against the wall. He stomped out, disappearing into the first-floor hallway. *Whew*, I thought. *Mason sure picked the right costume for the gala.* After all, Ares was the fierce, aggressive god of war—not someone you wanted to run into in a dark alley.

Taking a deep, silent breath, I waited a few seconds before making my way down the stairs to where Daniela was still standing, her eyes burning a hole through the door that Mason had just left through.

"Oh, hello again, Daniela!" I said brightly.

Daniela jumped a little at the sound and turned to see me. Recognition flickered in her eyes. "You're the girl from the gala, aren't you?" she asked.

I nodded. "I'm staying with Iris Pappas and touring the campus. I'm considering applying to Oracle next year, but I wanted to see it in action first."

Daniela looked uncomfortable. "Right . . . um, you didn't hear anything from upstairs, did you?"

I made my face as blank as possible. "No," I lied. "Why?"

"Oh, it's nothing," Daniela answered, visibly relieved. "Actually, I'm just on my way to visit Bash at the hospital. I know he's still unconscious, but they say hearing familiar voices help people wake up."

She was starting to turn away, but I reached out and touched her on the shoulder. "I don't want to hold you up, but would you mind answering a couple of questions about the school? I want to know what it's really like—can't always trust what's in the brochures, you know?"

Daniela smiled politely. "Sure, I'd be happy to," she said.

"Thanks. So, I really want to join a sorority, but all those hazing stories really freak me out. Do the Greek groups on campus do that sort of thing?"

Daniela shook her head. "I've never heard of that happening here—Oracle is a very serious school, not a lot of time for partying and getting in trouble." She chuckled. "We don't even have a football team—our big sport is chess."

"That can still be pretty competitive," I commented.

"Oh yes, don't get me wrong," Daniela replied. "Oracle is *very* competitive. Students vying for grants and scholarships, stuff like that. Unless you're like Bash and you can't help being the best." She sniffed, and blinked rapidly.

"You must like him a lot," I said carefully. "I'm hoping my boyfriend and I can attend college together. He's special too—so much more of a gentleman than my last boyfriend." Of course, this was a lie. I've only ever had one boyfriend. He goes to River Heights University and is a total gentleman, but I had a feeling saying this would help Daniela open up.

Daniela nodded furiously. "Right? You met my ex back at the gala. Mason. He won't leave me alone! He's had it in for Bash ever since we broke up. Always trying to one-up Bash or make him look bad, like it would matter if he did. I don't know what's wrong with him." She sighed. "Anyway, it was nice running into you again. Hope you like the rest of the campus!"

I waved good-bye and quickly exited the building. Suddenly that "prank gone bad" theory sounded a lot more probable. Outside, I pulled out my phone and started a text to Iris. FIND OUT EVERYTHING YOU CAN ABOUT A CLASSICS STUDENT NAMED MASON, I wrote. HE JUST MADE IT TO THE TOP OF MY LIST OF SUSPECTS.

CHAPTER FIVE

The Feathered Philosopher

I WAS EATING A SANDWICH IN THE COMMONS later that afternoon when my phone buzzed. GOT SOME INTERESTING INFO FOR YOU, Iris's text message read. MEET ME AT THE CLASSICS BUILDING IN 15. After finishing up the last of my lunch, I gathered up my things and walked over to the classics building on the west side of the campus. On the outside, the four-story red-brick structure looked very much like every other academic building at Oracle, but once I walked through the doors, it was abundantly clear what the people were there to study. The front vestibule was festooned with posters for PhD programs in ancient studies, and a large plaster bust of Aristotle stood on a pedestal in the center of the room.

A few students, on their break in between classes, were hanging out in the hallway comparing notes and sipping coffees from Drinx. One of them wore what looked like an athletic T-shirt, but on the back it read TEAM SOCRATES. I couldn't help but smile. On the wall next to the stairwell, a white marble plaque was set, engraved with a quote from Plato's *Republic*. "'The beginning is the most important part of the work,'" I read to myself.

I was mulling over the meaning of those words when the door of the building slammed loudly, making everyone in the hallway jump. I turned to see Dr. Stone rushing toward the stairwell, a steaming coffee cup in one hand and a thick packet of files cradled in the other. Her gray-white braids were loose this time, and she wore a magenta-and-gold African print dress, tied with a matching sash in the back. In her haste, she failed to notice the files sliding out of her grip, and before I could say a word of warning, they spilled onto the floor with a crash. "Oh—!" Dr. Stone exclaimed, probably biting back a curse as she surveyed the mess.

"Let me help you with that," I called out. I knelt at the professor's feet and began assembling the papers back into a neat pile. Most of them were student papers, all covered in handwritten comments and edits in purple ink.

Dr. Stone bent down to pick up the rest, and she gave me a strained smile as I handed the files back to her. Her skin was shiny with perspiration, and her hands shook as they held the papers. "You're that girl from the gala," she said matter-of-factly. "You asked me if I was all right, and I was abrupt with you. And now, here you are, being kind once again to the mean old professor you've probably heard so much about. Why?" She looked me square in the face, as if anticipating how I might respond.

Out of the corner of my eye, I could see the other students who had been loitering in the hall slink away, clearly wanting to avoid being caught in Dr. Stone's crosshairs. Pushing away my sense of unease, I took a deep, cleansing breath and thought about her question. After a moment, I said, "I don't reserve kindness only for people who are nice to me. And I don't believe everything people tell me. I like to make judgments for myself."

Dr. Stone's eyes crinkled with genuine pleasure, and she nodded. "You seem wise beyond your years—" She paused, lifting her eyebrows in a question.

"Um, Nancy. Nancy Drew."

"Dr. Stone. It's a pleasure to officially meet you. You've got a good head on your shoulders, Nancy," she said, shaking my hand. "And good heads are hard to come by nowadays." She gave Aristotle's bust a little pat, like it was a puppy. "And to answer, truthfully, your original question from the gala: no, I am not entirely all right." She seemed to deflate at that confession and wiped the growing perspiration from her temple. "Now, this has been a pleasant chat, but I must get to my office. . . ." She made for the stairwell once again, her steps shaky.

I darted forward to take the files back from her hand. "Why don't I carry those things for you—just until you get upstairs?"

Dr. Stone looked affronted for a moment, but then relented. "You certainly are an impertinent young woman," she said grumpily, but I could see a sparkle in her eye as she said it. A few moments later we'd reached the second floor, and Dr. Stone opened the door to her office. The room was an exercise in orderliness. Not a paper was out of place, not even a single pen cast aside on the desk—graded papers all lay stacked neatly in an out-box, and a platoon of uniform red pens stood at attention in a wooden cup next to the computer. Even the books that took up an entire wall, I noticed, were shelved according to subject matter and labeled with handwritten stickers—suggesting that Dr. Stone created her own library system for her collection. Dr. Stone entered the room briskly and bent to snatch a lone sticky note from the floor where it must have fallen. "Excuse the mess," she said, throwing the offending note in the garbage.

The only thing that did not fit into this picture was the large silver cage in a corner of the room. It was occupied by a steel-gray parrot, who was busy grooming the red feathers of his tail when we walked in. "Hello, Sophocles," Dr. Stone said, her voice softening with affection. The bird's head perked up immediately at the sound of his mistress, and he began hopping from one foot to the other in excitement.

"Agatha! Ya! Ya! Ya!" the bird said.

I looked questioningly at Dr. Stone, who replied, "Sophocles knows how to speak English *and* Greek phrases. 'Ya' means 'hello.'" Dr. Stone pulled a peanut out of her purse and handed it to the parrot, who took it and began tearing into the shell with his beak. "Good boy," she said, giving him a nod of approval.

"What kind of parrot is he?" I asked.

"African gray," Dr. Stone replied. "One of the smartest birds in the world. He's family, you know? I've had him for ten years now, but he's still just a baby. For all I know, the little rascal may just outlive me."

"Outlive you!" Sophocles crowed.

Dr. Stone smiled. "Not with that mouth, you won't." Sophocles responded to this by bowing his head toward the professor.

"He really loves you," I observed.

Dr. Stone nodded solemnly. "Sometimes I think he may be the only creature at this school who does," she murmured, almost to herself.

Stepping away from the cage, the professor dropped her papers and bag onto the desk and let herself sink into a plush chair, indicating that I should close the door. Curious, I did as I was told and then sat down in a chair across from her. After wiping a bead of sweat from her brow, she opened up her purse and pulled out an insulin pen from a plastic case and looked at me warily. "I don't usually do this in front of people," she said. "Correction, I *never* do this in front of people. But I just tested my glucose after class, and my levels are little low. . . ." She trailed off, looking uncomfortable.

"Oh! Of course, I understand," I said. "I have a friend in school who is diabetic; she has to have an injection once a day. Would you like some privacy?"

Dr. Stone's face relaxed. She seemed happy to be relieved of the burden of explaining her condition. "You can stay," she said. "It will just take a moment." I noticed that her hand was shaking slightly—she must have waited a little too long! She unsheathed the needle, and I felt my heartbeat quicken. I had never been a big fan of needles, and I always looked away when my friend gave herself the injection. But something about Dr. Stone's decision to let me stay made me feel like I shouldn't look away—shouldn't even flinch. *Was all that bluster downstairs some kind of test?* I thought. With the syringe poised above the bare skin of her arm, I wondered if this was a test too.

Dr. Stone didn't so much as blink as she stuck herself with the needle and injected the insulin. I gulped and tried to keep my face impassive. Meanwhile, my stomach was turning in somersaults. When it was done, she rubbed her arm for a moment and readjusted her dress. "Well! That's that," she said brusquely, and pulled a bag of candies out of her desk drawer. "Lemon drop?" she asked, popping a candy into her mouth and offering the bag to me.

"Sure, thanks," I replied. For a few minutes we sat in companionable silence, each of us sucking on our lemon drop. I noticed Dr. Stone's shaking hands become still, and her whole demeanor soften. "Your blood sugar was low at the gala, wasn't it?" I said after a while. "That's why you looked so unwell."

Dr. Stone cleared her throat. "I was foolish," she said, not meeting my eyes. "I dashed straight from my evening class over to the gala, stopping just long enough to take my injection and change into my costume. But once I got to the mansion, I was so overwhelmed by the crowd and the noise . . . I just forgot to eat. I'll admit, I'm notorious for forgetting to check my levels and administer injections. Sometimes my colleagues have to remind me on days when I'm particularly crabby!" She reddened slightly when she said this. "Anyway, when you saw me at the gala, the symptoms of hypoglycemia had started to hit me. The shakes, the dizziness—I should have gone straight to the buffet table, but I suddenly realized I was expected upstairs to prepare for my speech—"

I had been listening passively to her story, but at those words I suddenly became focused. "Wait," I interrupted her. "What do you mean, *your* speech? Bash was the one up on the balcony last night."

Dr. Stone sighed. "Yes," she replied. "But it *was* my turn to give the address this year. However, when Bash saw me stagger upstairs in such a pitiful state, he was very concerned for my well-being." She smiled a little at the memory and shook her head. "I had a glass of juice—that usually helps—but that night is just wasn't enough. I was still pretty shaky when it was time for the speech, so Sebastian offered to give it instead. I was too weak to argue with him, so I just went back down to my table and sat to watch him speak." She looked out of the window then, her lips pressed into a hard line. "In a way, that boy is in the hospital because of me."

"You can't blame yourself for what happened," I told her, my words coming out with more ferocity than I had intended. Dr. Stone looked over at me, eyebrows raised. "What I mean is," I continued, more evenly this time, "if I blamed myself every time the people I love suffered because of my actions . . ." I opened and closed my mouth, uncertain how to end that sentence. "Well, let's just say that I'd have a hard time sleeping at night. What happened to Bash is not your fault."

"Not your fault!" Sophocles squawked, startling us both. I stifled a giggle, and suddenly the tension in the room was lifted.

"So you're some kind of feathered philosopher now, are you?" Dr. Stone said to the parrot. "I suppose it's only right that you live up to your name." The professor sighed and turned back to me. "I guess you're right, Nancy. I couldn't possibly have predicted that passing off my speech would put Sebastian in danger. I just can't help but wish it were me in that hospital bed, instead of him."

At that moment, something clicked in my brain. I stood up, my mind awhirl.

"What is it?" Dr. Stone asked, her brow furrowed in concern.

"'The beginning is the most important part of the work,'" I said as pieces of the puzzle fell into place. "I had it all wrong from the start."

"Nancy, what in the world are you going on about? What does Plato have to do with Sebastian's accident?"

"Everything," I replied, and consulted the clock on my phone. "I'm sorry to leave so abruptly, Dr. Stone, but I'm late for a meeting. Perhaps we can continue this conversation later tonight, after your last class?"

The professor barely had enough time to agree before I was out the door and dashing down the stairs and back into the front hallway of the building. Iris was standing near the front door, looking at her phone. She glanced up at me as I approached. "Finally!" she exclaimed. "I was just in the middle of texting you. Where have you been all this time? I have important information!"

"Let me guess," I replied, still catching my breath. "Mason can't be our guy because he's got an alibi for the time the balcony was sabotaged."

Iris's eyes widened. "You *are* Sherlock Holmes! How did you know?"

"Just a hunch," I answered. "I already knew Mason wasn't the one, so I figured you were coming to give me a reason why not. Iris, I've been wrong about everything."

"What do you mean?"

"Bash wasn't the target of the sabotage—he just ended up being in the wrong place at the wrong time. Dr. Stone was the one who was supposed to give the speech. That fall was meant for her."

Iris lifted her hand to her mouth in shock. "Oh my gosh," she breathed. "So that means—"

"It means it's not over," I said. "Until we find the person behind all this, Dr. Stone is still in danger."

CHAPTER SIX

The Lightning Rod

A MOMENT AFTER I UTTERED MY REVELATION about Dr. Stone, the doors to the classics building opened and a wave of students began flowing in. Iris pulled me to the side to avoid the crush of people. "The next set of classes will be starting soon," Iris said over the din. "Let's go back to the mansion where we can at least hear ourselves think!" I nodded weakly. Suddenly I didn't feel so well at all. The noise and the crowd were making my head spin. I hurried to follow Iris outside.

Ten minutes later we were standing in the grand foyer of the president's mansion. With no events happening in the house today, we were alone, and it was blissfully quiet. I began to breathe easy once more, though I still felt wretched.

Iris plopped herself onto one of the upholstered armchairs placed in the center of the foyer, depositing her heavy book bag on the floor. "Nancy," she said. "I'm your friend, so I'm going to be honest."

I cringed. *She's mad that I led her on a wild-goose chase after the wrong person,* I thought. "I'm sorry," I spluttered. "I know I screwed up. We've been going about this case all wrong, and it's my fault."

Iris looked surprised. "Actually, I was going to say that salmon isn't really your color"—she tipped her chin toward my blouse—"but wow. Girl, it was an honest mistake! Don't be so hard on yourself! How were you supposed to know that Bash wasn't the target? I sure didn't."

I crossed my arms. "I should have spoken to the gala organizers right away. Any one of them could have told me that Bash doing the speech was a last-minute change." I glanced over at Iris, who was rolling her eyes in that familiar *oh Nancy* sort of way. It was how she always looked when we were kids and I was fussing over some insignificant mistake I'd made, like overcooking the marshmallows over the fire, or coloring outside the lines. I sighed and threw up my hands. "All right. Fine. I guess it's better that I figured this out now rather than even later. But still—I have a lot of catching up to do. Whoever sabotaged the balcony is probably already formulating a new plan to hurt Dr. Stone. We need suspects, and we need them now."

Suddenly a thunderous voice echoed through the room from above.

"Suspects, eh?"

Iris and I jumped at the sound, and I looked up to see a hulking figure standing in the shadows at the top of the staircase.

"Daddy?" Iris said.

Papa George emerged into the light, his expression stern. "Keeping secrets from your father, are you?" he boomed. "Never a wise choice." He was no longer in his gala costume, but Papa George still gave off the air of a god descending from atop Mount Olympus as he came down the stairs toward us. If Zeus were ever to wear a three-piece suit, I expected that was how he would look. It was intimidating, to say the least.

"Dr. Pappas—" I began once he was standing in front of me.

"Don't 'Dr. Pappas' me, Little Fox." He stopped me short. "I am well aware of your amateur detective work, and I would appreciate being kept apprised of any alleged mysteries on my campus before you start sticking your nose where it may not belong. What happened to Sebastian was an accident—nothing more!"

I cast my gaze toward Iris, who was attempting to make herself as small as possible—which, for a girl who was five foot eleven, was a real challenge. I set my jaw and tried to keep my voice level. "Papa George, I'm sorry we didn't tell you about all this earlier, but I wanted to follow up on my hunches before saying anything. The balcony *was* sabotaged, of that I'm sure.

But I think Bash's involvement was the accidental part. I now have reason to believe that someone was planning to hurt Dr. Stone during the gala, as she was the one who was supposed to be standing on that balcony. Who did it or why, I have yet to discover, sir. But I intend to."

"How can you be so certain?" he asked.

"Nothing is certain," I replied carefully. "But if there's even a slight chance that I'm right, then it means the safety of one of your professors is being threatened. Isn't that worth the risk?"

Papa George remained silent, his blue eyes boring into mine. I tried not to flinch. Finally he let out a long breath and relaxed. "You always were a tenacious little girl, Nancy," he said, his voice softer now. "I see nothing has changed." He pulled at his beard, his expression thoughtful. "Come into my office, both of you. Tell me everything you know, and I will be the judge of whether your 'case' has merit."

Papa George turned on his heel and began making his way down a hallway toward the back of the mansion. Iris, standing back up to her full height, gave me an approving wink before pulling me along with her in his wake. "Nice going, Drew," she whispered in my ear. "I should keep you around for when I get caught staying out past curfew."

I rolled my eyes and smiled. Little did Iris know how my heart was racing! Thank goodness Papa George decided to give me a chance. He could have easily sent me home packing, and then the case would never be solved. Now I just had to convince him.

Papa George's office was like a museum of Greek antiquity. The walls were covered with one painting after another of scenes from Greek mythology, and in one corner, a statue of Perseus fighting the gorgon Medusa stood on a wooden pedestal. The artist had sculpted the hero's face to have an expression of courage laced with abject terror. I thought, at that moment, that I knew exactly how he felt!

Papa George sat down in the maroon Queen Anne armchair behind his desk, filling every corner of it with his girth, and laced his fingers together over his chest before looking at me. "You may begin," he said.

I took a deep breath. *Well, here goes nothing.*

Five minutes later, I finished my briefing of everything that had happened since the gala. Papa George's lips were pursed as he mulled over all the evidence. "All right, Nancy," he said. "Given all that you've told me, I'm willing to go along with this"—he paused— "investigation, but only to a point. You may talk to people to gather information, but you are not to mention your suspicions to anyone. If word gets out that I'm allowing a high schooler to play private eye on my campus, I'll be a laughingstock. If you get a lead or find new evidence, let me know immediately. Do not, for any reason, put yourself in unnecessary danger. Is that understood?"

"I understand," I replied. After all, understanding something isn't the same as promising not to do it. Given all my past experiences, promising to avoid dangerous situations was pretty much like a swimmer promising not to get wet.

"If it's all right, Papa George, I'd like to start with you," I said.

"Me?"

"Of course. After all, you know more about the professors and students on this campus than anyone. Who do you think would have a reason to hurt Dr. Stone?"

Papa George's brows furrowed at this, and he cast his eyes around the room as he sat, deep in thought. He picked up the long silver lightning bolt he'd used as part of his costume from where it was leaning against his desk, studying it for a moment. "Agatha," he began, "is a woman like no other. Unapologetically opinionated, fiercely bright; she storms into meetings and classrooms, questioning everything, uprooting the status quo, always questing for ways in which we can be better. For this, she has admirers, and I count myself as one of them. But unfortunately, her outspokenness and her constant demand for excellence has also made her many enemies. She is a real lightning rod, always attracting negative attention for her high standards."

Putting the walking stick back down, Papa George regarded me once more. "That is to say, you'll have no shortage of suspects, Nancy. You've got your work cut out for you figuring out which one is your culprit."

Knowing what I already did of Dr. Stone, I'd been afraid of this. But I didn't allow myself to get discouraged—I'd cracked tough cases like this before. "It's one thing to be upset at a professor for something like a bad grade," I said thoughtfully. "But to actually set out to hurt her? To create such a complex plan? What kind of person would go to such lengths, over something so trivial?"

Iris snorted. "Trivial? Ha! You obviously haven't been at Oracle long enough, Nance."

"What do you mean?" I asked.

"Oracle kids are intense—and I mean *really* intense—about their GPAs. A huge percentage of the students go on to places like Stanford and Princeton for their doctorates, so the stakes are very high and the competition is fierce. A bad grade—even one—is anything but trivial."

"Well," I said, "then I think a visit to a couple of Dr. Stone's classes may be in order."

"Fine," Papa George said with a nod. "But remember, keep a low profile. With the classics chair still unfilled, the last thing I need is more dramatics around here." As had happened yesterday when I'd first spoken to Papa George, the same dark clouds gathered in his expression as he said this.

"Cameron Walsh's post, you mean?" I asked, remembering the name Iris had mentioned, Papa George's old friend who had died recently. I spoke softly, knowing I was treading on unstable ground.

Papa George looked up at me, his eyes glistening. He cleared his throat and answered, "Yes—yes, that's the one. Big shoes to fill, Cameron's are. Not an easy man to replace. Your Dr. Stone is at the top of the list, actually. Between her impressive credentials and her long history with Oracle, she certainly is qualified. But I'm just not ready to make the decision yet. Some of the faculty seems to think young Dr. Brown would be an excellent choice, but I'm not convinced of that. He certainly has charisma, and a brilliant mind, for sure—but without a significant publication or two under his belt, I simply don't think he's up to the task." Papa George chuckled. "For all I know, Dr. Brown's social calendar may be so busy that he wouldn't have the time for such stuffy things as administrating. He seems to enjoy the spotlight of the classroom!" *Hmm,* I thought. *Could the culprit be someone on the faculty who'd rather work for Dr. Brown than Dr. Stone?* I filed the idea away for later consideration.

Papa George glanced at his gold wristwatch and started. "Oh, look at the time! Well, Madam Detective, are you finished with me? There are some things that I need to attend to."

I smiled. "Yes, that's good for now. Thank you for believing in me, Papa George."

The college president rose out of his chair and pointed a finger in my direction. "Don't thank me yet, Little Fox. If you and that daughter of mine stir up trouble, you'll be out on your tail faster than you can say 'spanakopita.'"

"Understood," Iris and I said in unison.

She snickered. "It's like being in fifth grade all over again!" she whispered to me as her father made his way out.

"Shh!" I hissed. Once he was gone, I added, "Can't even wait until he's out of the room to make a comment, can you?"

Iris rolled her eyes. "Oh, pooh. You thought it was funny too. Listen, Dr. Stone has an ancient philosophy course starting in half an hour. One of my friends is in that class, and she's always complaining about how hard it is. If we hurry, we might be able to make it there before the class starts!"

"Perfect," I said. "Do you think it's possible that one of the faculty members might be our culprit? From what your dad said, it sounds like there might be people out there who wouldn't want Dr. Stone as chair."

Iris shook her head. "The professors are a bunch of peace-loving bookworms. I can't imagine one of them doing something like this. But the students?"

She shrugged. "I think it's possible. It *is* a competitive school. It wouldn't be completely crazy to think that one of them might be determined enough to try and take out the toughest grader on campus."

I nodded. "Okay, let's scope out the class and see what we find." Picking up my bag from the floor, I started making my way out of the office when a painting on the wall behind the door caught my eye. It depicted a tall woman holding a bow, her gaze fixed on a white stag in the distance. Behind her, a huge crescent moon glowed in the night sky. It was a striking image that spoke of strength and solitude. The goddess's face reminded me of a certain other woman, who I'd seen staring thoughtfully into the night. "Isn't that—?"

"Artemis," Iris completed my thought. "Goddess of the moon. She's the one that Dr. Stone was dressed up as for the gala."

"I thought so," I said. "I wonder why?"

Iris shrugged. "It makes sense to me. Artemis was probably the most fiercely independent of all the goddesses. She was so dedicated to nature and the skill of the hunt that she made Zeus swear that she'd never have to marry. She didn't care about what anyone else thought. She just did what she loved."

"Huh," I said. "That *does* sound a lot like Dr. Stone."

As we walked back out toward the quad, I wondered about the parade of gods and goddesses I'd seen at the gala the night before. How many others dressed up as a character that reflected themselves? If only I could look at a costume and see their true intentions within it. But even if I could, the gods themselves were anything but simple—anything but just purely good or purely evil. Even the goddess of beauty had a dark side. Even the god of death wanted love. No, I didn't need a villain; I needed to find the person who'd want to see Artemis fall.

The goddess of the hunt was being hunted—and I needed to find out why.

CHAPTER SEVEN

~

Know Thyself

THE SKY OVER ORACLE COLLEGE WAS A fiery collage of oranges and reds as the sun began to set. Iris and I were walking across campus to sit in on Dr. Stone's ancient philosophy class. The air had that telltale smell of autumn, a combination of earth and smoke. On the way, we passed by Dr. Brown, who looked even more handsome in regular clothes than he did in his Apollo costume. His brown hair was swept stylishly to the side, and his tortoiseshell glasses complemented his brown vest and slacks perfectly. He was chatting animatedly with a few students, who all seemed to hang on his every word. "A B average is fine for some, I suppose," he was saying. "But to truly be great, you must aim *higher*. As Heracleitus once said, 'Big results require big ambitions.' You must not allow obstacles to prevent you from following your path to greatness." The wide-eyed students nodded, some of them even taking notes.

"Yeesh," Iris groaned as we passed by. "Those girls act like he really is a god. Give me a break. I never understood the whole hot-for-teacher thing."

"I bet you'd change your tune if he was talking about the difference between chambray and denim," I said with a smirk.

Iris raised the back of her hand to her forehead and fluttered her eyelids dramatically. "Ohh," she swooned. "Be still my beating heart!"

Dr. Stone's ancient philosophy class was in a huge, curved lecture hall inside one of the academic buildings on campus. There must have been at least a hundred seats, and they were rapidly filling up by the time Iris and I arrived. We entered at the top tier and nabbed two seats on the aisle, where I had a good view of the students in front of me. Guilt has many ways of expressing itself—in body language, tone of voice, choice of words. I wanted to make sure that if guilt showed its face, I'd be there to see it.

"Look!" Iris said, pointing. "There's Dr. Stone."

I gazed down toward the front of the class to see Dr. Stone striding into the room. Unlike when I'd seen her earlier, she radiated a commanding presence that caused the people in the room to fall quiet almost immediately. Students who'd been loitering in the aisles quickly took their seats, pulling out laptops and notebooks from their bags. Dr. Stone arranged her own papers on the podium and checked her wristwatch. My phone read 5:59 p.m.—one minute until the class began. As the time clicked over to six o'clock, I saw Dr. Stone clear her throat and face the class. "Good evening," she intoned, her rich voice filling every crevice of the hall. "Before we begin, I have an announcement to make. Sometime this afternoon, my African gray parrot escaped from his cage in my office."

I gasped. Sophocles? But I'd just seen him a few hours ago. Poor Dr. Stone, she must be devastated. I watched her carefully, but whatever the professor was feeling at that moment, she was hiding it well.

"He is a very smart bird, so it's possible he unlatched the cage himself and left through the open window," she added. *Hmm*, I thought. *Could the missing bird have something to do with the threat against Dr. Stone? Perhaps he didn't just escape. Perhaps . . . someone took him.* I decided I needed to return to Dr. Stone's office to search for clues.

"Regardless," Dr. Stone continued, "I'm asking all of you to please keep your eyes open on campus and let me know immediately if he is located." She paused for a moment, looking down at her pile of papers, as if she might find her beloved pet within them. "He is . . . very valuable to me. So whoever returns him will be rewarded."

Then the professor cleared her throat and opened her three-ring binder with a snap of finality. "All right, then. Today we'll be discussing one of the oldest maxims in ancient philosophy—"

Just then the slam of a door interrupted Dr. Stone's lecture, and a hundred heads swiveled to see who it was. A pale, gangly young man slouched into the front of the room, making a beeline for a single empty seat in the corner. But Dr. Stone's clarion voice stopped him cold.

"Mr. Bosco, how nice of you to join us."

The kid's face turned pink almost instantly, and some of the students tittered. He started to sit down, but Dr. Stone stopped him once more.

"Wait a moment, Mr. Bosco. I think you might be able to help me. I'm trying to introduce our topic for the day." Reluctantly, the kid stayed standing, shifting from foot to foot as he waited for Dr. Stone to continue. "As I was saying, class, we'll be discussing the ancient maxim that was inscribed in the Temple of Apollo at Delphi: 'Know thyself.' Two words. Seems simple, yes?" Dr. Stone glanced at the Bosco boy, who nodded. "Ah, but those two words contain multitudes, and have been attributed to a dozen Greek sages and used again and again for thousands of years. So, what does it mean? Mr. Bosco?"

The young man's eyebrows furrowed in thought. "I guess it means it's important to know what kind of person you are."

"Very good," Dr. Stone said. "And why should that be so?"

Mr. Bosco looked puzzled, but after a moment, he said, "If you don't know what kind of person you are, you won't make good decisions for yourself. Like, if you don't know that you're someone who hates crowds, you might decide to move to New York City and be really unhappy there."

"Indeed," Dr. Stone said, pleased. "Or if you don't know that you're someone who tends to be tardy, you might end up being late to class three times in one week."

The young man blushed again and bit his lip in embarrassment.

"Thank you for your gracious assistance with the lesson, Mr. Bosco. You may sit now."

"Wow," I whispered to Iris as the young man hurriedly took his seat. "She's brilliant."

Iris nodded in agreement. "She is. But not everyone

appreciates her teaching style. She doesn't take kindly to kids trying to coast through her classes. For all we know, any one of the students in here could be our culprit."

As Dr. Stone delivered her lecture, I scanned the room, looking for any sign of suspicious activity. My gaze zeroed in on a couple of young men a few rows down from where we were sitting. They were a few seats apart and one of them was trying to inconspicuously show the other something on his phone.

"Mr. Wilcox, Mr. Rogers," Dr. Stone said, her eagle eyes on the two young men. "I had thought Friday's warning not to use your phones again during my class would have been sufficient, but I see I was wrong. Please bring your phones to the front of the classroom, I will give them back to you before class on Wednesday."

"What?" the blond kid asked, his palms upraised. "That's crazy, Professor!"

"Perhaps, Mr. Wilcox," Dr. Stone said. "But this course is only for those students who take their studies seriously. And since you are insisting on behaving like high school students, it seems I must treat you as such. "

The two young men were still for a moment, their faces slack in disbelief, before they walked to the front of the room and handed her their phones. I overheard the blond one mutter, "She's not going to get away with this."

I looked at Iris to see if she'd heard him too. Her wide-open eyes told me she had.

Dr. Stone continued the lecture as if nothing had happened. I noticed she liked to lean into the podium to emphasize certain points. *Anyone familiar with her classes could assume she would use the balcony railing during her speech,* I thought.

Later in the period, I saw the guy named Rogers try to pass a note to his friend. I nudged Iris and she rolled her eyes in response.

Not surprisingly, Dr. Stone saw it too. "Gentlemen, I hadn't counted on your resourcefulness in the face of actually having to pay attention. I see you've resorted to the old-fashioned way. Well, I have had enough of these distractions in my classroom. You may both take an unexcused absence for the day. Good evening."

They boys stuffed their things back into their bags and scowled at the professor. As Rogers stood, I spied the note they'd been passing sticking out of his back pocket. Thinking fast, I turned to snatch the water bottle from Iris's purse. "Can I borrow this?" I asked.

"Um, sure," Iris whispered. "Does sleuthing make you thirsty?"

I didn't answer. I was busy watching the two guys come my way up the aisle, and trying to get my timing right.

Just as they were passing by, I knocked the bottle of water off my desk. It hit the floor and splashed all over the Rogers kid's shoes. "Oh my gosh!" I whispered, wary of attracting the wrath of the professor myself. "Sorry, I'm such a klutz."

The young man sighed, aggrieved, and bent down to pick up the bottle. As soon as his pocket was exposed, I plucked the note from it and secreted it in my lap before he stood up again. "Here you go," he muttered, handing the bottle back to me.

"Thanks so much," I said quietly, flashing him a smile.

Once they were both gone, Iris leaned over to me. "Clever girl," she whispered. "Now what does it say?"

I held my breath and unfolded the paper.

"Well, fiddlesticks," Iris said.

"It's all Greek to me," I quipped, and Iris shot me a dirty look.

"Oh, ha. Very funny, Sherlock. I was hoping for an actual clue, but instead we got somebody's homework."

On the paper were a few lines of text written in Greek. Which, given where we were, wasn't so surprising. It looked totally innocuous, just like someone's half-completed assignment. "Is it homework, or maybe an encoded message?" I said. Could it be that those two guys were planning something? What the Wilcox kid said about Dr. Stone "not getting away with" humiliating them sounded pretty threatening. I'd have to translate the note to find out for sure.

"That's it for today, class," Dr. Stone was saying. "Please read chapters four and five on the Socratic method for Wednesday. Good night."

The students rose almost in unison from their seats and began chatting and gathering their things. "I need to speak with Dr. Stone," I told Iris. "Why don't you talk to some of the other students and see what they know about Wilcox and Rogers? It doesn't sound like this is the first time they've had a run-in with the professor. See if you can get a little background on them."

"Yes, ma'am," Iris said, saluting. "I'll meet you back at the mansion later tonight."

I made my way down the aisle to the front of the lecture hall, where Dr. Stone was packing her messenger bag with notes and binders. She looked up when I approached and chuckled. "Are you writing an unauthorized biography about me, Nancy, or are you just interested in the classics?"

"The latter," I said with a grin. "Although I would be interested in reading the former if someone were to write one."

"Flattery will get you nowhere," Dr. Stone said with a wink. "Now, what can I do for you?"

"I was sorry to hear about Sophocles," I said. The sparkle left the professor's eyes almost instantly, and she looked back down at her bag, a few of her gray-white braids falling in front of her face. "I wanted to offer my help in finding him. I've got a lot of experience . . . locating missing things."

Dr. Stone quirked one eyebrow at that. "And how, may I ask, do you propose finding my bird?"

"I'd like to come back to your office and look around a bit, since it was the last place he was seen. I may find clues there that will point us in the right direction." Dr. Stone looked skeptical. "If there's a chance it could help, isn't it worth trying?" I added.

"Appealing to pathos, are you, Nancy?" Dr. Stone sighed. "All right. Fine. Come to my office tonight at nine. I have a few late meetings before I'm done for the day."

I smiled and nodded.

"But I'm warning you, Nancy—no mumbo jumbo.

If you start talking about auras and crystal balls, we're finished."

"No mumbo jumbo," I repeated. "Got it."

At nine o'clock on the dot, I walked up to the classics building, alone. Only the lighted windows of the classrooms and offices inside pierced the deep blue night, and I pulled my cardigan tighter around me as a chill wind crept across my neck.

Iris, who had some kind of club commitment that evening, had pleaded with me to take an escort, but I wouldn't hear of it. "It's okay," I'd told her. "I can take care of myself!"

Iris had looked unconvinced. "Uh-huh. I've heard how much trouble you get yourself into." She shook one manicured finger at me. "Don't make me call Bess and George on you, Drew! I know how stubborn you can be, and I'll have both of them shouting in your ear if need be."

"Please don't," I sighed. "I *promise* you, Iris—it's just a quick trip to Dr. Stone's office, and then I'll be back before you know it. I'll text you when I get in."

"Fine," Iris agreed. "But I'm not happy about it."

"Obviously," I said with a grin.

Now, a few hours later, I was opening the door to the building and stepping inside the empty corridor. It was utterly quiet. An anxious feeling prickled up my spine as I began climbing the stairs to the second floor.

What are you getting all jittery about? I asked myself, my footsteps echoing in the open space. *It's just an empty building. There's nothing to be afraid of.* I took a deep breath and quashed the feeling, focusing on the task at hand. *Dr. Stone is in her office, waiting for me,* I thought. *I doubt she's afraid.*

But Dr. Stone's office was dark.

I tested the doorknob, and it was unlocked. Figuring she was just running late, I opened the door and groped along the wall for a light switch. After a moment or two without success, I remembered that there had been a banker's lamp on the desk, and I made my way through the gloom to find it and switch it on. It didn't illuminate the whole room, but it helped drive away the shadows enough that I could start investigating Sophocles's cage. The first thing I noticed was the number of feathers on the floor surrounding the cage. There had only been a few this morning—now, little gray feathers were scattered in a wide radius around the cage. *There was a struggle,* I guessed. Birds didn't normally lose this many feathers that quickly, even if they were molting—a fact my childhood parakeet had taught me. I wondered why the normally neat Dr. Stone hadn't cleaned up the mess, but then again, she'd been distressed and probably not behaving normally. Sometimes when people lose something they love, they're hesitant to move anything from where that loved one last left it.

Next, I looked at the latch on the door of the cage and noticed something else. It looked perfectly fine. No scrapes or scratches in the rubber coating on the bars. If Sophocles had engineered his own escape, there would be evidence of his sharp beak and claws at work here. It was just as I'd feared: someone—possibly the same person who'd sabotaged the balcony—was making another plan to hurt Dr. Stone.

Suddenly a strange, screeching noise broke the silence. It seemed to be coming from outside and sounded something like, "So sauce on! So sauce on!" A thought struck me: Could it be Sophocles? It certainly sounded like a parrot, and I had already seen Sophocles talk. Maybe I was totally wrong about his being kidnapped, and he had returned home!

I dashed to the window—it was slightly ajar so I pushed it all the way open. It sounded like Sophocles was somewhere below. Pulling my phone out of my pocket, I switched on the flashlight and shone it outside, leaning out as far as I dared.

"So sauce on!" I heard again.

Cooing, I leaned out a little further in hope of luring him up to the window. I still couldn't see him. *Maybe he's afraid and hiding in the bushes*, I thought.

Without warning, the rug beneath my feet gave out. I lurched forward, my heart in my mouth, and my hands scrabbled for purchase in the open air. But it was no use. Before I could even draw breath to scream, I was falling.

CHAPTER EIGHT

Occam's Razor

LATER, I WOULD TRY TO REMEMBER JUST how I grabbed onto the window after falling headfirst through it. But all I know is that it involved a sort of somersault that left me hanging from the sill by my fingertips, my back against the building. I strained to hold on as my feet struggled to gain purchase on something. Luckily, the uneven brickwork of the building created indentations in its face, just deep enough for the edge of my heels to rest on.

Precariously balanced, I hazarded a glance down at the ground below—it was about twenty feet to the grass. If I landed on my feet, there was probably a 50 percent chance I could survive the fall without serious injury. However, I could also break a leg or a hip on impact. If I fell on my back, those chances dropped precipitously. People have died from falling only ten feet if they landed the wrong way. All in all, though, if I played my cards right, I'd probably survive the fall.

Of course, "probably" isn't a very reassuring answer when it comes to whether you're going to live to see tomorrow.

"Help!" I finally managed to scream. "Someone come quick!" I scanned all the windows in the classics building for movement, but they were all dark.

My fingers were beginning to get slippery with the cold sweat of panic. My wrists ached from their awkward position. I could feel my fingers slowly sliding off, the muscles in my hands and arms locking up. I had only a few seconds left.

Just as my arms were about to give out, I heard a rustling coming from above me. I looked up and shouted, "Is someone there? Please—I can't hold on much longer!" A few agonizing seconds passed, and then someone appeared in Dr. Stone's office window, silhouetted by the light coming in from behind.

"Nancy?!" the figure said, and I recognized the voice.

"Dr. Brown!" I exclaimed. "Oh, thank goodness!"

With great effort, the young professor leaned out the window, grabbed my hand, and hauled me back into the building.

For a few minutes, I just sat on the Persian rug, trying to take deep breaths and waiting for my pulse to stop racing. Dr. Brown stood nearby, his handsome face pale and glistening with sweat. "Are you all right?" he asked, wringing his hands. "Should I call an ambulance?"

"I'm fine, thanks to you," I replied, rubbing my sore arms. "Just a few scrapes from the brick, that's all." I peered at the edge of the rug nearest to the window, which had bunched up where I had fallen. "It's so odd how it happened, though. I thought that the rug must have slipped out from under my feet where I was leaning over, but it looks like there's a rug pad under here to stop that from happening."

Dr. Brown studied the rug too. "How very strange," he agreed. "Although the maintenance people do wax the hardwood floors now and then, which makes them quite slippery. If you were leaning out very far, it could be that even the rug pad wasn't enough to stop it from slipping."

"I suppose," I said. "Anyway, it was lucky that you were here—otherwise, I might have really needed that ambulance!"

Dr. Brown rubbed his neck and shrugged. "Oh, well, I only did what any Good Samaritan would have done. I had just come up to my office to pick up some papers when I heard you shout for help."

"What is going on here?" Dr. Stone was standing in the doorway, looking tired and confused to find two people loitering inside her office.

"Dr. Stone!" I said, quickly getting to my feet. "I can explain." I quickly told the professor about coming in to examine Sophocles's cage and how I thought

I'd heard him calling from outside. Dr. Stone's eyes grew wide when I got to the part about falling out the window.

"So," she said when I'd finished. "It looks like you're quite the hero, eh, Fletcher?"

Dr. Brown colored and cleared his throat. "Not at all, not at all," he said humbly. "I just happened to be in the right place at the right time." He turned back to me and gave me a dazzling smile. "Well, young lady, I am very glad you're all right. I'll leave you to your meeting." With that, he bowed and left the room, and I couldn't help but notice how well his suit seemed to fit.

"Get in line, Nancy," Dr. Stone said as she set down her things.

"Huh?" I asked, snapping out of my reverie.

"You look like you got one of Cupid's arrows right between the eyes," she replied with a smirk. "But you're not the only one. The majority of this department's student population is head over heels in love with that young whippersnapper. I suppose I can see the allure. He is attractive and charming."

"I can feel a 'but' coming on . . . ," I said.

Dr. Stone chuckled. *"But,"* she continued, "he's always focusing on the wrong thing. He finds students like him—the charismatic crowd-pleasers—and puts them up on a pedestal, telling them to be 'the best' and fight their way to the top of the heap. Whatever that is. That's just not my way. I find that often, it's those studious, diligent students who keep their heads down and really *do the work* that succeed." She paused, thoughtful. "It's like Euripides said: 'The good and the wise lead quiet lives.' At least, that's what I believe." She sighed. "Anyway, I like Fletcher. He's cute. If you like that sort of thing."

"He prevented me from falling out of a second-story window," I said. "What's not to like?"

Dr. Stone shook her head. "It boggles the mind. And if I hadn't been late getting up here after class, it could have been me leaning out that window! Two near falls in just a couple of days—what do you think of that? Either I've got terrible luck, or someone's out to get me."

I knew she was joking, but the truth of what she said hit me all at once. What had just happened to me *was* a lot like what had happened to Bash at the gala! Again, it happened to the wrong person, but both times it seemed like Dr. Stone was the intended target. I might be right about the rug not slipping on its own—maybe Dr. Brown wasn't the only one in the building. In the dim light, someone could have mistaken me for Dr. Stone.

Someone who wanted to pull the rug out from under her. Literally.

It was her office, after all; they wouldn't expect anyone else to be here at this hour. More than that, only a person who knew about Sophocles would have stuck their head out the window in response to his call. But now that I thought about it, I hadn't seen any bird when I'd been hanging on for dear life. And I'd scanned the entire building when I was searching for a rescuer—even if he'd flown off, I would have seen some sign of him. Had Sophocles's call been a trap? It made sense, but then, where was he now?

Realizing I'd been quiet for too long, I glanced back at Dr. Stone, who was gazing out the still-open window. "You know, after we lost Cameron, I thought I'd be done with loss for a while. But it looks like loss and I aren't finished with each other yet. Poor Bash. That boy has potential. I hope to God he comes out of that hospital the same as he went in."

"Cameron Walsh," I said. "The old classics chair. You and he were friends?"

She nodded, a nostalgic smile spreading across her face. "That old coot was even grumpier than I am. Always stomping around the building in the same ratty old suit jacket, pieces of his lunch still lodged in his beard. He never cared about appearances—never had the time for that. He was too busy being a genius."

"You must have admired him," I said.

"Oh, I did. And I like to think the feeling was mutual. We worked together for many years, Cameron and I. We squabbled like an old married couple, but it was a fruitful relationship. We helped each other. Before he died, he'd been working on a paper about one of Protagoras's lost texts. It was a big deal, really hush-hush. I was honored when asked me to read it. I think I was the only one who did."

"I'm so sorry," I said. "Whatever happened to the paper?"

Dr. Stone shrugged. "I don't know," she admitted. "Cameron hated computers, so it's probably buried among all those files that we boxed up after he passed. No one has had the time to go through his things for the archive yet. I'm sure it will turn up." She sighed. "I just wish he'd have been here to see it published."

With a sigh, she walked over to Sophocles's cage and picked up a box of birdseed from the shelf. She was about to pour a little into his feeding bin when she stopped herself. "I always give him a little dinner before heading home for the night," she said sadly, setting down the box again. "I guess old habits die hard."

"We'll get him back," I promised.

"You said you heard him outside the window," she said. "At least that means he's still alive. Maybe he got scared off and he'll come back again tomorrow."

"Maybe," I lied, remembering my discovery about the cage. Everything was still leading me to believe that Sophocles had been birdnapped. "Speaking of that, there's something I wanted to ask you. When I heard him, it wasn't just squawking—it seemed like he was saying something, possibly in Greek. It sounded like, 'so sauce on.' Do you know what it means?"

Dr. Stone raised a hand to her mouth. "Yes—yes, I do. He's saying *zdeú sōson*. The direct translation is 'Succor, oh mighty Zeus' and I trained Sophocles to say it when he needs help."

I swallowed hard.

"If he just got out of his cage, why would he be calling for help?" Dr. Stone asked.

"Well," I answered, "it *could* be that he was frightened from being outside alone. . . ."

Dr. Stone skewered me with a calculating stare. "I can feel an 'or' coming on," she said.

Guilty as charged. "*Or*," I continued, treading carefully, "he could have been calling for help because someone was keeping him from coming home."

There was a pregnant pause as the professor took in this revelation. She cleared her throat. "You think someone . . . *kidnapped* my parrot?"

The way she said it made it sound like this was a truly ludicrous notion. *Uh-oh,* I thought, alarm bells going off in my head. Something told me this wasn't going to go well. Desperate to explain myself, I told her about the lack of claw or beak marks on the door to the cage, and how unlikely it was that he'd have been able to open it without leaving some behind. "It's still possible, of course," I added. "Just . . . not probable."

Dr. Stone crossed her arms, clearly not convinced. "Who would do such a thing? And why?"

"I'm still trying to figure that out," I admitted. "Do you have any idea who might have a grievance against you? A disgruntled student, perhaps?"

The professor's eyebrows rose. "Am I that hated, then?" she asked, her voice suddenly harsh. "Do the people you've met here detest me so much that you think they'd go to such lengths just to hurt me?"

I hesitated, unsure how to answer such a loaded

question. Obviously, I'd hit a nerve. "I didn't mean to suggest that. I just . . . I just think it's possible that someone might have taken Sophocles on purpose, to use him against you. And I'm—"

"Occam's razor, Nancy," she broke in. "The simplest answer is usually the right one. A bird goes missing from his cage. Most likely, he opened it and flew away." She walked to the office door and stood by it. "I think it's time for you to go."

I squeezed my eyes shut in frustration. This wasn't the way I'd wanted this meeting to go! But there was nothing for it now. I gathered my things and walked out the door. I looked back at her to say something more, try to salvage the evening, but she held a hand up, and the words died on my lips.

"I should never have agreed to let you come here," Dr. Stone said, shaking her head. "I allowed my fear for Sophocles to delude me into thinking that you actually might be able to help me find him. But I should have taken my own advice. If something sounds too good to be true, it probably is."

And with that, she closed the door.

I stood there for a minute, staring at the gold name-plate morosely. As investigations go, this one wasn't going well. First I zeroed in on the wrong victim, and now I'd alienated the real one! Dr. Stone might still be in danger, but even if I told her as much, she'd never believe me. Someone tried to hurt her again tonight, and almost put me in the hospital in the process. Who knew when the next attempt might be?

I had to make some real progress, and fast. For Sophocles—and his beloved professor—I had a feeling that time was running out.

CHAPTER NINE

~

The All-Seeing Eyes

I WAS SITTING IN MY ROOM IN THE MANSION, moonlight spilling through the window overlooking the campus beyond. Suddenly something white and tied with a string was pushed under the door.

What could that be? I wondered.

I went to pick it up and unrolled the note, which was on thick, rough paper that almost felt like parchment. Somehow I knew that what was written there was important—maybe even essential to solving this mystery. But when I looked at the paper, it was covered in Greek writing. I couldn't understand a word of it.

I felt a surge of frustration rise in my chest. Nothing was making sense! Who would write such a message? I ran to the door and threw it open, hoping to catch the person who'd delivered it.

But the person standing there wasn't a person—at least not in the normal sense. It was a man-shaped creature, wearing a black robe, and every inch of its body was covered with staring eyes.

"*Open your eyes,*" the creature said, its voice reverberating in my head.

I said nothing, struck dumb with awe and terror.

"*Open your eyes,*" it said again, "*and you will find the answers you seek.*"

The creature opened its mouth again, but this time, instead of words, a buzzing sound came out, like the sound of a horde of bees humming in a repeating rhythm.

Buzz. Buzz. Buzz.

The insistent vibration dragged me awake, and I sat up in bed.

I blinked at the daylight in my room, confused—but relieved. It had just been a weird dream, and the buzzing sound was my phone. A *very* weird dream. But my relief lasted only a moment. Instead of being home in River Heights, I was still in my guest room in the president's mansion—mired in an investigation that had been going nowhere. "Ugh," I said, flopping back onto the pillow. I wasn't ready to deal with reality just yet.

But reality wasn't going to let me go back to dreamland. My phone, which was still ringing incessantly, was about to throw itself off the nightstand. I caught it just as it vibrated itself over the edge and gazed blearily at the screen. GEORGE FAYNE, it read, and displayed a photo of George giving me a toothy grin and two thumbs-up.

"Hello," I croaked.

"Well, hello to you too, sunshine," George said. "It's a little late to still be in bed—especially for you! How's it going over there?"

"Oh, just peachy," I replied, clomping over to my suitcase to try and find clean clothes.

"Drew, sarcasm does *not* become you. What's wrong, gumshoe? Can't put your finger on the goon? Stuck behind the old eight ball? Some cat not being square with you?"

"You think you're funny, but it's not funny."

"It's a little funny."

I sighed and tried not to smile. "Okay, fine. It's a little funny." While I got dressed, I brought her up to speed with everything that had happened since she and Bess left. "So that's where things stand," I finished. "I'm almost certain someone is trying to hurt Dr. Stone, but I still don't know who or why. There are plenty of students who have motive—she's probably handed out plenty of bad grades in her day—but I have no way of narrowing them down or proving that they had the opportunity to sabotage the balcony before the party or kidnap her parrot. And as for whether someone pushed me out of her office window—I was in the classics building, so any one of the students in the department could have known about her office hours and been there at the right time."

"Huh," George said thoughtfully. "I see your problem." There was a pause as both of us racked our brains, trying to come up with a solution. "Wait a second," George said suddenly. "The cameras!"

"What?" I asked.

"The security cameras in the president's mansion! I noticed them when we first came into the building. They're those white spheres that look like little eyes— pretty sophisticated technology. They're only the size of your palm, so they're easy to miss."

Open your eyes, my dream had told me. Maybe this was what the creature meant.

"I bet you they take digital video surveillance," George continued. "And the files are kept somewhere on a server. If you review the files from the day of the gala, you'd be able to check who came in and out of the mansion during the time when the balcony was sabotaged. That would help you narrow down your suspects!"

"George, you're a genius!" I said, feeling a spark of excitement reigniting inside my head. "Thank you so much!"

"Sure thing, doll," she replied. "If you need any more help, just drop me a dime, savvy?"

"You are so weird, George," I said.

"Please come home soon," George whispered into the phone. "Gramps's computer has been updating for forty-eight hours straight and *I am so bored*."

After promising that I would do my best to wrap up the case quickly, I washed up and went downstairs to find Iris.

"I thought you said you had a key to this room," I murmured as I watched Iris wiggle a credit card into the crack of the locked door.

"I meant a key in the general sense," Iris replied, biting her lip in concentration as she jimmied the card farther into the locking mechanism. "Like, an object capable of unlocking the door."

"Uh-huh," I said, unconvinced. I was about to

suggest that I work on the door instead—as I've had plenty of experience—but I decided to keep my mouth shut. Iris seemed intent on contributing to the case, and I wasn't about to get in her way.

I eyed the small red sign on the door, which read, in no uncertain terms: AUTHORIZED PERSONNEL ONLY! It was late afternoon now, and we were down in the bowels of the president's mansion, which was a lot darker and dustier than it was upstairs. All around us in the musty hallway were large rolling bins piled with dirty linens, carts filled with cleaning supplies, and stacks of extra chairs and tables for events. The door Iris was so industriously trying to open was to the security office, which held all the servers and computers that controlled the house's surveillance cameras.

"Got it!" Iris exclaimed in triumph as the door popped open.

"Shhh!" I warned. I thought I heard the sound of footsteps in the distance. Even though Iris was the president's daughter, I couldn't be sure we wouldn't be tossed out on our ears if we were caught snooping around inside the security office.

"Oh, sorry," Iris said, ducking her head. "*Got it!*" she whispered.

I rolled my eyes. "You know, Iris—the thing about being a spy is, you *don't* want people to notice you!"

Iris glanced down at her outfit, which today consisted of an attention-grabbing yellow-sequined A-line dress, making her look like the world's most glamorous hazard sign. Beautiful, but not exactly subtle. "Oh, don't be such a worrywart, Drew. If someone catches us, I'll just distract them with my irresistible charms and then you can bop them on the head with a vase or something! Isn't that what you people do?"

"There will be no bopping of heads, Iris!" I whispered, exasperated. "Now get inside before someone sees us!"

The security office was a small, claustrophobic room cluttered with shelves of humming, blinking electronic equipment. The floor was littered with cables snaking from one end of the room to the other, where they converged onto a sleeping computer on an old desk. I quickly took a seat at the desk and tapped at the keyboard until the screen came to life. Lucky for me, the computer wasn't password protected, so within a few minutes I was deep into the surveillance video files, searching for the right one.

"Here it is!" I said. "The day of the gala. If we check the recordings for both the front and back doors of the mansion, we should be able to see every person who entered and exited the building that day. The person who sabotaged the balcony would *have* to be one of those people!" Iris pulled up a chair next to me, and we both perched at the edge of our seats and fast-forwarded through the videos, pausing only when a figure appeared in the video. Most of the people to appear were catering staff carrying in food and supplies for the gala—I felt comfortable eliminating those people as suspects. Other than me and the girls, the only people who came into the building were a couple of professors—Dr. Brown and one of the adjuncts—who Iris said had come to supervise the setup of the guest seating.

"They do it every year," Iris added. "Whoever gets the two short straws has to do the job."

I nodded, but frustration was building in my chest again. "There's still a bit more video left to watch," I said, and we continued fast-forwarding. "Wait!" I said as a dark blur flashed on the screen. I clicked back a few minutes, and sure enough, a figure in a blue hoodie emerged into view. As I clicked forward by the second, the figure moved closer to the camera. Finally, the person looked up at the camera, and in that one frame, I could see his face. A face I recognized.

"Mr. Wilcox!" I exclaimed. "It's that boy from Dr. Stone's philosophy class! The one who was kicked out with his buddy while we were there. He's certainly got motive. And now it looks like he's got the opportunity as well."

Iris nodded. "Caught him red-handed," she said with a grin.

"Well, not quite," I said. "The mere fact that he entered the building doesn't prove anything. We need to catch him in the act. But how?"

We both sat in thoughtful silence for a moment. "Wait a second," Iris said. "What about that note you pinched from his pocket? We never did figure out if it was just homework—or something more."

"Gosh, you're right!" I exclaimed, rummaging through my bag. "With everything else happening, I'd completely forgotten about it! Aha—here it is." I unfolded the crumpled paper and looked again at the Greek writing. "Hmm, I wonder if this computer has Internet." With a few clicks, I'd found a translation website and began carefully transcribing the English translation of each word onto the paper.

"What does it say?" Iris asked when I was done.

"Well," I replied, "it's certainly not homework. It says: 'Meet me in the professor's office. Tuesday at eight.'"

Iris's eyes widened. "That's tonight!"

I refolded the paper and placed it back in my

bag. "They could be trying to make another move in Dr. Stone's office. I have to go. It might be my only chance to catch them in the act and prove their guilt!"

Iris searched my face. "You're doing this alone, aren't you?"

I nodded. She must have seen that determination in my eyes. "As much as I'd love you to be there, Iris, I think I have a better chance of success if I'm by myself."

"Okay, but you better keep your phone with you. Don't be a hero, Drew!"

"I won't," I promised. "Just don't say anything to anyone yet. Until I know for sure that our hunch is correct, we don't want to start making accusations."

"Roger," Iris agreed, saluting.

After putting the computer back to sleep and locking the door behind us, Iris and I snuck back up to the main level of the mansion. "Well, I've got to run to my last class," Iris said breezily. "Good luck, Sherlock!" She turned away, but then paused and looked back at me. "Seriously, though," she added, her voice laced with tension. "Be careful, okay?"

"Don't worry," I replied. As I watched her go, I inwardly hoped that I had sounded more confident than I felt.

It was already dark by the time I found myself standing in front of the classics building once again. I shivered as I looked up at Dr. Stone's darkened office window, thinking about how close I'd been to falling out of it. The thought of falling made me think of Bash—I wondered how he was doing. He must not have regained consciousness yet, or else I would have heard about it. I made a mental note to ask Iris about him once I got back to the mansion.

I checked my watch: seven forty-five p.m. I wanted to get inside and find a good hiding place in Dr. Stone's office before the boys showed up. I started toward the front door but was startled when a figure suddenly arose from the bushes. "Oh!" I exclaimed.

It was Dr. Brown. He looked about as startled as I was, with a couple of leaves and twigs stuck in his hair.

"Nancy!" he said. "My goodness, we just keep running into each other, don't we?"

I felt my face redden. "Um, yes, I guess we do," I answered. Somehow, he looked just as handsome littered with shrubbery as he did normally. Apparently I had a weakness for bookish types! Thank goodness my boyfriend Ned couldn't see me now. "Did you lose something in the bushes?" I guessed.

"Actually, yes," Dr. Brown said. "My dictation machine!" He held up a small recording device, which looked a bit dirty and scuffed. "I noticed it was gone this morning and I've been frantic all day! I have all my notes for lectures recorded on it. Luckily, I found it right here in the bushes. Must have fallen out of my bag on the way to class."

"That is lucky," I agreed. Realizing that I needed to get inside quickly, I bade Dr. Brown good night.

"Good night, my dear," Dr. Brown replied. "Be careful out there!"

He walked briskly away, and I walked up to the door. *Well,* I thought as I entered. *Here goes nothing.*

CHAPTER TEN

❧

On Truth

A FEW MINUTES LATER I STOOD BEFORE Dr. Stone's office door—again—hoping both that it would be unlocked and that this would be the last time I'd have to visit it. I reached out to grasp the doorknob when suddenly the door flew open of its own accord.

"Nancy!" Dr. Stone said when she saw me. She was wearing a khaki overcoat and carrying all her bags. She was obviously on her way out, and from the way her things were hastily thrown together, it looked like she was in a hurry. "What are you doing here?"

I froze, woefully unprepared for the possibility that

she would still be here. *Her last class ended hours ago! Why does my target have to be such a workaholic?* "I—well," I stammered, my mind racing. "I came to apologize. For yesterday. I'm sorry for upsetting you. That was never my intention."

Dr. Stone's eyes softened a little. "Well, that's very kind of you, Nancy. But I'm afraid I can't linger—I've just received an e-mail from someone in the next town over. They've found Sophocles!"

My mouth dropped open. "Really? Are they sure it's him?"

Dr. Stone gave me a sidelong look. "How many African gray parrots do you know who can speak fluent Greek?"

"Not many."

"We're meeting up in the parking lot of the Cornucopia Supermarket in half an hour. It'll be so good to finally have him home!" She smiled, her eyes sparkling with excitement. "Anyway, I'm sorry to have disappointed you, Nancy. No thrilling kidnapping scheme this time." The professor pulled out a fist-size bunch of keys, locked the door, and bustled off down the hall and out of sight.

I stared at the locked door and muttered a curse. Dr. Stone had poked yet another hole in my theory with her story of Sophocles's imminent homecoming. If I was wrong about him being taken by the culprit, what else was I wrong about?

My existential crisis was interrupted by the sound of two voices. Male voices. And they were coming my way. I needed to hide before the rest of my plan went up in smoke! I jiggled the knob of the janitor's closet next to Dr. Stone's office, but it was locked too. The office to the left? Also locked. The voices were getting louder. I had to move, fast! Desperate, I ran to the opposite side of the hallway and tried that office door—and miracle of miracles, it opened. I glanced at the nameplate before dashing inside—it was Dr. Brown's office.

I closed the door almost all the way, keeping it open just a crack so I could have enough light to get an idea of my surroundings. Unlike Dr. Stone's pristine working space, Dr. Brown's office was a jumble of papers, textbooks, scholarly journals, and half-empty cups of coffee. The only orderly thing in the room was the wall behind his desk, where the professor's various degrees and certificates of excellence were artfully hung. Before I could make any further observations, I heard footsteps approaching and peeked cautiously out the door.

Sure enough, it was the guys from Dr. Stone's class, right on time. I pulled out my phone and fumbled with it in the dark, trying to get it to start recording. I needed proof, after all.

"I still can't believe that old crone took away our phones in front of everybody. She's got a lot of nerve," said the blond boy, Wilcox.

"Someone should really bring her down a notch," said the other boy. It wasn't easy to look menacing with freckles, but this kid did his best. I wondered what kind of sabotage they were going to try next—I had to catch them in the act.

I waited for them to turn to Dr. Stone's office and

try the knob, but instead they turned the other way, right toward me!

I scrambled back from the door and shuffled, on all fours, across the carpet before diving underneath Dr. Brown's desk. And not a second too soon. A moment after I'd pulled myself into the darkest corner of the desk, the office lights flicked on. They were inside.

But why? I thought in confusion. *Why are they coming in here?*

To my horror, they were approaching the desk where I was hiding. I pulled myself as far into the dark recesses as possible, willing myself to be invisible and trying not to breathe. Had they seen me? Had I been caught?

But no. It seemed that Wilcox and Rogers were searching for something—and that something wasn't a nosy detective. "Where did Dr. Brown say he would leave them?" Wilcox asked.

"He said he put them in his desk for safekeeping," Rogers answered. "But then again, he is supposed to be here, I mean he's always here at this time. And he told me he would hand them off tonight when we talked this morning. I wonder where he is?"

"Who knows? Anyway, he left his door unlocked, so maybe he meant for us to just come in and find them ourselves." After rummaging through a couple of the desk drawers, Rogers opened the long middle drawer right above my head. As he did so, I heard a soft peeling sound, after which an object fell right into my lap. I froze, thinking that the sound would cause Rogers to search under the desk for the source—but luckily, he was distracted by whatever they'd found in the drawer.

"Here they are!" Rogers said. "Man, look at all these texts I got."

"Yeah, and about two hundred e-mails," Wilcox added. "Dr. Brown is the best! I knew running all those little errands for him before the gala would pay off. As soon as Dr. Stone took our phones away, I was sure I could count on him to get them back for us. I scratch his back, he scratches mine."

"C'mon, let's get out of here," Rogers said, moving back toward the door. "I've got so much to catch up on."

A few seconds later the lights were switched off and I heard the door click shut.

In the darkness, I banged my fist against the floor in frustration. That was it? The mysterious meeting was just so they could retrieve their cell phones from Dr. Brown's office? I found it odd that the strict Dr. Stone would agree to allow their phones to be returned earlier than she planned, but Dr. Brown must have managed it somehow. The man seemed to have a knack for ingratiating himself with people—whether it be with charisma, charm, or even a little favor like this one. It was quite a skill.

And as for my incriminating footage of Wilcox sneaking into the mansion in his hoodie hours before the gala—that was a bust too. He'd just been running innocuous errands for Dr. Brown, and probably wearing the hoodie because of the bad weather, not because he was trying to hide something. Another dead end.

After turning off the video on my own phone, I switched on the flashlight feature and crawled back out from under the desk. The object that had fallen into my lap turned out to be a file folder full of papers— not surprising, given the general disorganization of Dr. Brown's office. I stood up and set the folder on the desk next to a vase of yellow flowers. They smelled so sweet and pungent; I thought they must have been delivered very recently.

A card lay next to the vase, and, my curiosity getting the best of me, I decided to take a peek. Could it be from a secret admirer? I was certain the professor must have plenty of those. Turns out, it *was* from an admirer, but not the kind I'd imagined.

Dear Fletcher, the card read. *I thought a little color would brighten up your day—hope you like them. I hardly need to tell you how excited all the editors here at* Prometheus *are about your paper "The Lost Truth." New discoveries with lost texts are so rare, and so we expect a big response to your paper in our publication! That said, we were hoping to have it in hand first thing Monday, but we haven't seen anything from you yet. If we still are looking to include it in next month's issue of the journal, we will need it ASAP. Here's hoping you'll be sending it over soon! All best, Ellen Underwood, Senior Editor.*

I set the card back on the desk, my body tingling all over. Pieces of this puzzle were finally falling into place.

The lost truth. The answer to this mystery had been staring me right in the face this whole time, but until now, I just hadn't seen it. But knowing it wasn't enough—I needed proof. But how could I expect it to just fall into my lap?

Unless it already had.

I snatched the file folder back up from the desk where I'd set it. Each of the four sides sported a strip of masking tape. *That was the peeling sound I'd heard when Rogers opened the drawer!* I thought. *The folder hadn't been stuffed inside the drawer and gotten stuck—it had been taped to the bottom of it.*

The question was: Why would you tape a folder underneath your desk, unless it was something you didn't want anyone to find?

Inside the folder, I found a long typewritten paper, covered in handwritten notes and comments. It told me everything I needed to know.

I looked at my watch—half an hour had already passed since I stood at Dr. Stone's door. Stuffing the file folder into my bag, I dashed out of the office and the building, taking a shortcut through the open field to the parking lot where I'd left my car. As I threw myself into the driver's seat, stepped on the gas, and sped off down the road out of campus, I hoped that I wasn't already too late.

CHAPTER ELEVEN

Too Close to the Sun

THERE WASN'T A SINGLE OTHER CAR IN sight as I careened down the dark country road. The silent, still world all around me felt at odds with the alarm bells going off inside my head. The parking lot where Dr. Stone had told me she was going to pick up Sophocles was only a mile away now. I should get there in time. . . .

But then the unthinkable happened.

My car ran out of gas.

"No, no, no, no, NO!" I cried as the engine sputtered and died. I leaped out of the car, scanning the horizon for signs of life. But if there was a gas station nearby, I couldn't see it. And anyway, I didn't have time for that. There was only one thing to do.

Run.

I took off down the road, shining my phone's flashlight ahead so I could see where I was going. With my bag thumping rhythmically against my back, I sprinted around twisty turns and under thick canopies of trees, where the buzzing of cicadas was almost deafening. After a few minutes, my legs and lungs were screaming at me to stop, but I kept on going. After cresting a hill, I could see the store in the distance, a long, low building with a large parking lot out front. A few streetlamps lit up the lot, which was empty save for a single car.

No, scratch that. There was something else in the parking lot. Something small. I squinted at the thing, which only came into focus once I got a little closer. It was a cage. And something was moving inside.

Sophocles!

Someone was getting out of the car now. Someone

wearing a very familiar khaki overcoat. Dr. Stone, leaving her car door wide open, ran toward the cage and knelt down beside it. If I had been nearer, I might have heard her cooing at her bird, telling him how much she missed him and how happy she was to see him. But I was still a hundred yards away, and despite my desperate prayers to Hermes to let me borrow his winged shoes, I was slowing down.

A moment later, movement in the shadows of the storefront caught my eye. A figure, all dressed in black and wearing a hood, emerged from the murk and began approaching Dr. Stone from behind. She was so immersed in her reunion with Sophocles that she must not have been paying attention, because she stayed kneeling at his cage.

The figure was almost upon her now. Mustering all my strength, I raced toward them, closing in on the last bit of distance between us.

Faster! Go faster!

Suddenly the figure raised his arm, and I saw something gripped in his hand that glinted in the lamplight.

Finally, I was close enough to scream.

"*Stop!*"

Dr. Stone leaped to her feet in surprise, and then, seeing me rushing toward her, looked utterly confused and said, "Nancy?" But the dark figure was undeterred. He lunged at her with the thing in his hand.

"Behind you!" I cried, and threw myself at her attacker. Dr. Stone dodged out of the way, leaving the figure and me to land on the asphalt in a heap, my hands and knees scraping painfully into the gravel. The thing in his hand skittered across the ground—an insulin syringe.

The attacker shoved me off and got quickly to his feet. He started to make a run for it across the parking lot, but not before I could raise myself to sitting and shout, "There's no use running, Dr. Brown. It's over."

The dark figure stopped in his tracks and stood with his back to us for a moment. But then he turned around to face us and pulled off his hood.

"Fletcher?!" Dr. Stone exclaimed in shock. "What were you—? Why—?" She then turned to look down at me and say, "Nancy, I demand you explain to me what's going on here!"

"I'm sorry to have to tell you this, Dr. Stone, but these accidents that have been happening around you lately—Bash's fall at the gala, Sophocles going missing, and me tumbling out of your office window—they weren't accidents at all. Dr. Brown orchestrated them, and they were all meant to hurt *you*."

Dr. Stone looked stricken and turned to face Dr. Brown. "Fletcher, this isn't true . . . is it?"

Dr. Brown didn't answer. His handsome face had twisted into a grotesque mask of rage and fear and disbelief. He was shaking visibly as he finally opened his mouth to speak. "How did you know?" he asked me.

"For a long time, I didn't," I confessed. "In fact, I barked up quite a few of the wrong trees. But it all came together when I found this." I pulled the file folder that I'd found in Dr. Brown's office out of my bag and showed them both the lengthy paper inside.

Dr. Stone pointed at it, surprised. "Where did you find it? That's—"

"The late Cameron Walsh's unpublished paper, yes. The note from your editor, Dr. Brown, mentioned that the title of the work you were submitting was 'The Lost Truth,' and it reminded me of what Dr. Stone said about the paper Dr. Walsh had been working on before he died. A big discovery about one of Protagoras's lost texts. Once I saw this paper— which is written about Protagoras's *On Truth*—I knew it was one and the same."

"But I thought it was buried somewhere in Cameron's things!" Dr. Stone said.

"It was," I agreed. "Until Dr. Brown found it. He probably discovered it when you were all cleaning up Dr. Walsh's office, realized what he was holding, and secretly kept it for himself."

"Why would he do that?" Dr. Stone asked.

"Because he knew that with Dr. Walsh gone, the classics department would need a new chair. And he very much wanted it to be him."

"I deserve it!" Dr. Brown broke in. "The students at this school worship the ground I walk on! The staff

~ 154 ~

loves me—and I have every academic honor imaginable. Why shouldn't it be me?"

"Because," I continued, "despite all of that, you didn't have the scholarship. Papa George said that you just needed a big publication to have it made—but you hadn't written anything of note yet. And knowing that, when you saw this major academic breakthrough fall into your lap, you knew you had to take it for yourself. Dr. Walsh was notoriously secretive about his work, and now he was dead. No one would be the wiser if you published it under your own name. Except there was one problem." I raised the paper and shined my light on it, so that they both could see it clearly. "This paper was covered in notes and comments, written in purple ink. That meant that one person had read it and knew that this was Cameron Walsh's work, not yours. And I'm guessing you identified that person because you knew that only one professor on campus uses purple ink on her papers: Dr. Stone."

Dr. Brown shook his head in disgust, and I knew that I was right.

"And knowing Dr. Stone, you knew she would blow the whistle on you the moment she saw the paper in the *Prometheus*. If she barely tolerates texting in her classroom, there's no way she'd let plagiarism of this severity go by. She was too ethical to be bought or convinced to keep her mouth shut. You knew that. So you needed to get her away from Oracle—by whatever means necessary."

Dr. Stone was silent as all this started to sink in. Now she didn't look confused—she looked angry. "Bash is in the hospital because of you? Because of this . . . blind ambition?"

The young professor wrung his hands in anguish. "I didn't mean for that to happen!" he said. "When I heard you were going to give the speech at the gala, I thought it would be the perfect opportunity to . . . get you out of the way. I went in early under the guise of helping with setup"—I nodded, remembering how Iris and I had seen him come in on the security feed— "sabotaged the balcony, and everything was good to go. But then I saw Bash up there, not you. I wanted to stop him, wanted to say something—but it would have given me away. So I kept my mouth shut and hoped for the best." He swallowed hard and wiped a film of sweat from his forehead.

"You coward," Dr. Stone growled. "You're lucky Bash is still alive!"

"You could have ended it there," I continued. "But the editors at the *Prometheus* were expecting your paper—and with Dr. Stone still in the picture, and not on some kind of extended medical leave, you couldn't send it. So you tried again." Dr. Brown's eyes flicked to the cage, where Sophocles was bobbing his head, seeming to listen to every word being said. "Yes, you decided to kidnap Dr. Stone's beloved bird. Using Sophocles as bait, you set up a trap in Dr. Stone's office, hoping to cause her to fall out of her office window looking for him. Another explainable 'accident.' But you didn't count on me showing up instead of Dr. Stone."

Dr. Brown sighed, and buried his face in his hands.

"You must have only realized the plan had gone awry when you heard me calling for help instead of

Dr. Stone. That's when you ran over, ready to play the role of the hero."

"What else could I do?" he asked. "I didn't want yet another injury on my conscience. It's not my fault you were in the wrong place at the wrong time."

Dr. Stone looked at her colleague with raised eyebrows. "Why, Fletcher," she said, sarcastically. "I never knew you were such a raging narcissist. Now you're blaming Nancy for almost getting hurt in a trap *you* set?"

"Well," I added, "his hero act worked very well to throw me off his scent. I never suspected him after that. But there was something later that stuck out as strange to me. When I ran into you rummaging around in the bushes on my way to the classics building tonight, you were looking for your dictation machine. You said it fell out of your bag that morning, but I think you put it there the night I fell."

"What? Why would you think that?" Dr. Stone asked.

"Because when I was hanging from the window

after hearing Sophocles calling for help, I didn't see your parrot anywhere. That's because Sophocles was never actually there. Dr. Brown must have recorded him talking on his dictation machine. He knew that you had late meetings that night and would return to an empty building. I'm guessing he waited outside until your light went on, pressed play on the recording and hid it in the bushes. He probably used something to magnify the sound. Knowing that you would lean out the window to listen for the bird, he ran up the stairs to literally pull the rug out from under you."

Dr. Stone blew out her cheeks. "Indeed, and quite creative, I'll give him that," she said.

"Once I knew that you were the person who had stolen Sophocles, I knew that Dr. Stone was in trouble tonight. You were running out of time to deliver your alleged masterpiece to the *Prometheus*, so in a panic, you devised this final plan." I bent down to pick up the tiny syringe from where it had fallen from his hands. "You knew you could lure her out here with a fake story and the promise of Sophocles's return. And you knew that Dr. Stone was diabetic and sometimes a bit forgetful when it came to her injections."

Dr. Stone gasped. "You were going to put me in a diabetic coma?"

Dr. Brown shrugged. "Probably only for a little while. It's just a small overdose, really."

"Just a *small* overdose?" Dr. Stone spluttered.

"In your best-case scenario," I said, "Dr. Stone would have been laid up in the hospital with no memory of the incident, and probably put on temporary hiatus. I guess that would give you the opportunity to get your stolen paper published, and, with Dr. Stone out of the running, you'd be the clear choice for chair of the department. But I still have one question, wouldn't there always be the chance Dr. Stone would read the article and know what you did?"

Dr. Brown balked at my accusing gaze. "You have to understand—I did it for the good of the school! For Oracle—and for the students! Agatha may be brilliant"—he gestured toward Dr. Stone—"but she doesn't have what it takes to lead! Passion! Charisma!

The ability to inspire young minds! And, deep down, I think Agatha knows this too. I was sure she only had to see how successful I was as the chair. I would explain everything to her and she would see that I am the best choice for the job, that I did the right thing. She would agree to keep my secret. For the good of the school."

I looked back at Dr. Stone, expecting to see her fuming at his pompous speech, but she looked solemn. "Hamartia," she whispered.

"What's that?" I asked.

"It's a term from Aristotle's *Poetics*. It refers to a fatal error or flaw made by a hero that eventually leads to a tragic end. One bad decision that starts a chain of events leading to his downfall." She looked at Dr. Brown, who seemed to wither like a sun-scorched flower under her burning gaze. "When you set out to steal Dr. Walsh's work, you started down a path to ruin. At that moment, you ceased to be the kind of man who was worthy of Cameron's position."

The words struck Dr. Brown like a blow. It was as if Dr. Stone, like Artemis herself, had aimed her arrow straight at his heart and drove the point home. Dr. Brown collapsed to his knees. "I—I—" he stammered. "I'm so sorry, Agatha."

Dr. Stone nodded, the moonlight shining in her eyes.

At that moment, the sound of a car engine roared toward us, and within seconds a large white SUV tore into the parking lot and came to a screeching halt, its headlights shining in our eyes. Dazzled by the glare, I barely could make out the two figures that jumped out of the car and approached us.

"Oh, Nancy," said Iris, her curly dark hair a wild halo around her head. "Thank goodness you're all right." Her cell phone was gripped in her hand—my flurry of text messages probably displayed on the screen. I'd told her where I was going and why as I was running to my car. "We came as soon as we could."

Papa George loomed over the crumpled figure of Dr. Brown, like a great and powerful god looking down upon a poor, misguided soul. "Fletcher, look at me," he commanded.

Dr. Brown squinted up at him, blinking into the blaze of light.

"Is it true?"

Dr. Brown hung his head. "Yes."

Papa George frowned, his craggy face wrinkling with disbelief. "But you had such a bright future . . ."

"I was so close," Dr. Brown moaned. "So close to greatness, I could almost reach it!"

"Greatness comes from small beginnings," Papa George told him. "It is not stolen from the hands of others. You flew too close to the sun, my friend. Now you must pay the price."

With a nod, Dr. Brown allowed himself to be led into the SUV. Before getting back in his car, Papa George asked Dr. Stone to help Iris and me retrieve some gas for my car while he accompanied Dr. Brown to the police station. "And Nancy," Papa George added, laying a heavy hand on my shoulder. "Thank you. I should have known never to doubt my Little Fox when she tells me there's villainy afoot. Oracle College owes you a great debt. There might even be a scholarship with your name on it—when you're ready."

I smiled. "Thanks, Papa George," I said. "I'll let you know."

Iris, Dr. Stone, and I watched them drive away into the night. As the sound of their engine faded into the distance, the growing silence was pierced by a squawking cry. "Mama!" it said.

"Oh!" Dr. Stone exclaimed. "My baby! How could I forget you?" She ran over to Sophocles's small cage and knelt down to open the door. The African gray parrot hopped out and onto her arm, side-walking up to her shoulder, where he nuzzled her with his beak and cooed. "Mama!" he repeated.

"Well, Nancy," Iris said, coming to stand next to me and watch the happy reunion. "Looks like this case is another feather in your cap. Get it? Feather? Because of the bird . . . ?"

I raised an eyebrow at her. "Your jokes are almost as bad as your spying skills," I said with a smirk.

"Yes, well," Iris huffed, "that may be true, but if

I'd been around, I would have told you those shoes are *not* appropriate for long-distance running or chasing perps." She indicated my black flats, which indeed looked the worse for wear. My feet didn't feel so good either.

"Touché," I agreed. "I guess that's why we make such a great team."

"Darn right, we do," she said, clapping me on the back. "Now, how about a late-night milk shake to celebrate our combined genius?"

"Great idea!"

CHAPTER TWELVE

Icarus Rises

GOING TO THE LOCAL HOSPITAL WASN'T
exactly on my list of things to do while visiting Oracle
College, but the afternoon after my confrontation with
Dr. Brown in the parking lot, that's exactly where I was.
Thankfully, the reason for my visit was a happy one.

Bash was awake.

I'd gotten a text message from Iris late that morning, after a long, dreamless sleep—she said she'd heard
from her father that Bash had regained consciousness
overnight, and was talking and answering questions
like his usual self.

After a quick breakfast, Iris and I jumped in my car and drove over to the hospital to see him. I walked through the automatic front doors, carrying a steaming cup of coffee in one hand and a bouquet of get-well-soon flowers in the other. "Ugh," said Iris, balling up the corner of her pink skirt in annoyance. "I knew I should have picked up a gift at the store. You're going to make me look bad."

"There's a gift shop inside," I told her. "You can always pick up a balloon or a stuffed animal or something."

"Do you think they have one shaped like a bust of Socrates?" she asked.

I wrinkled my nose. "A balloon or a stuffed animal?"

"Either?"

"Probably not."

She shrugged. "Alas. He'll have to make do with a box of chocolates, then."

As she sashayed over to the gift shop, I made my way to the elevator bank. When it arrived, I stepped in and pushed the button for the third floor. But just as the doors were closing, I heard a voice call out, "Hold the elevator!"

I shot my arm out to block the doors, and they automatically reopened. A woman ran inside, her long salt-and-pepper braids streaming out behind her. She was dressed in a golden yellow silk blouse and a high-waisted, ankle-length skirt, printed in a colorful geometric design. She looked like a bird-of-paradise in human form, or some other kind of tropical plant that made the ones in my hand look drab in comparison.

"Dr. Stone!" I said in surprise. "You must have heard about Bash as well!"

She nodded and smiled, a dazzling smile that lit up her entire face. "Yes, isn't it wonderful?"

"You look . . . different," I observed, not sure how to describe the transformation I was seeing. She looked like a new woman, more energetic and vibrant than I'd ever seen her before.

"Bash's recovery wasn't the only good news I received this morning," she said, her eyes sparkling.

"Dr. Pappas called first thing to ask me to be the new chair of the classics department!"

I gasped. "That's fantastic! Congratulations!"

Dr. Stone beamed. "Thank you. I can hardly believe it myself."

I pushed the button for the third floor once more, and we rode the elevator in comfortable silence for a few moments. I cast a look at the professor and noticed her biting her lip—a look of concern furrowing her brow. "What is it?" I asked. "You are excited about the position, aren't you?"

Dr. Stone looked up. "Oh—yes, of course. It's just . . . all those things Fletcher said last night, I can't get them out of my head. About how I don't have the ability to lead. That I'm brilliant but uninspiring. And now—I'm going to be the chair of the department! It's a well-known fact that I'm not the most popular woman on campus. What if he's right about me? What if I don't have what it takes?"

I shook my head. "Don't you remember what you told me back in your office? 'The good and the wise lead quiet lives.' That's you! The good and wise. You don't need to be everyone's best friend and biggest crush to be an inspiration. Just giving people what they want doesn't help make a difference in their lives. You push people to be better. They don't have to like it—but at the end of the day, I think they will really appreciate it." I put a reassuring hand on the professor's arm. "I think you're going to be great, Dr. Stone."

Dr. Stone smiled and nodded. "That's very sweet of you to say, Nancy," she said. But something in her eyes told me she wasn't completely convinced.

The elevator doors opened, and the professor and I walked down the hall to find Bash's room. "Ah, here we are," Dr. Stone said, and we walked slowly through the open door. There, surrounded by greeting cards, balloons, and flowers, was Bash.

He was dressed in a blue hospital gown and sitting up in his bed, his black, curly hair mussed from sleep, reading what looked like a heavy textbook. "Studying already?" Dr. Stone said with a chuckle.

Bash looked up from his book, and his eyes lit up at the sight of us. "Dr. Stone!" he exclaimed. "Oh, it's so good to see you!"

"Likewise, dear boy," Dr. Stone replied. "I was worried there for a while, but I knew you'd pull through this all right in the end."

"Hi, Nancy," Bash said, remarkably remembering my name. "So, what did I miss?"

Dr. Stone and I eyed each other. I blew out my cheeks and said, "A lot, actually." And with that, I began to regale him with the long tale of Dr. Brown's repeated attempts to put Dr. Stone out of commission. Bash's eyes grew larger with every passing minute, and halfway through the story, Iris arrived in the room with an embarrassingly large heart-shaped box of chocolates and began adding her own two cents to the account.

"And *that's* when we broke into the security office in the mansion!" Iris announced.

"You did *what*?" Dr. Stone asked, her arms akimbo.

Iris made an *oops* face. "It's fine, really!" she

reassured the professor. "It was all for a good cause! No files were harmed in the solving of this mystery!"

Dr. Stone humphed but let it go. By the time we finished the story, Bash was positively astounded. "Wow," he whispered. "Dr. Brown. I never would have thought he'd be capable of all those awful things! He always seemed like such a cool guy."

Dr. Stone looked somber. "Sebastian, I'm so sorry that your greatest mentor ended up disappointing you like this. I know that I would feel terrible if someone were to betray my trust like that."

Bash looked confused. "My greatest mentor? What do you mean?"

Now it was Dr. Stone's turn to look confused. "In the speech you made, the night of the gala—you were talking about your greatest mentor right before you fell off the balcony."

"Yes," Bash said slowly. "But I wasn't talking about Dr. Brown. Don't you remember? I never got to actually say who it was." He smiled. "I was talking about you."

Dr. Stone blinked. She stumbled back a step and laid a palm on her chest. "You . . . you were?"

Bash chuckled. "Of course! Why do you think I always stayed late after every one of your classes? Always came to see you during your office hours?"

"I—I just thought you were a diligent student, concerned for your grades . . . ," Dr. Stone stammered.

"Nah, I don't care so much about grades," Bash said with a shrug. "You're one of the only professors who doesn't just want to make me memorize facts and dates and theories. You make me *think*. Really think! About the meaning of life, the secrets of the universe—everything. That's why I want to know what you know. So I can be like you."

Dr. Stone's eyes were watery as she listened to Bash's words, and when he was done, she whispered, "Thank you," and patted him on the hand. She was quiet, but I could see that the sparkle had returned to her eyes.

"Well, it's been a great visit, everyone," I said. "But I think it's time for me to get back to River

Heights. My dad probably thinks I'm never coming back!"

After giving Bash a hug and telling him to keep in touch, I turned to Dr. Stone to say good-bye. "You know," she told me, "I never properly thanked you for everything you've done. Even after I practically threw you out of my office, you put aside your own personal safety to come to my rescue." She rummaged in her purse, pulled out a cloth bag, and placed it in my hand. "I can never truly repay you for your kindness, Nancy, but I wanted to give you this small token of my appreciation. Something I picked up many years ago when I was studying in Athens."

I tugged open the strings of the bag and pulled out a small pewter statue of a woman clad in long robes, holding a hand mirror aloft in one hand. Across the base of the statue, a single word was engraved ALETHEIA. I looked back at Dr. Stone, a question in my eyes.

"Aletheia is the goddess of truth," she said. "For a young woman whose life seems to be steeped in a never-ending quest for truth, I thought she would make quite a fitting gift."

I clasped my fingers around the figurine and smiled. "It's perfect," I told her, and slipped it into a special little pocket in my bag.

"I'll walk you out," said Iris, throwing her arm around my shoulders. We strolled together out of the hospital room, stopping at the elevator bank to exchange hugs and promises to call and write. "Oh!" she said with a start. "I almost forgot! I've got a little something for you too." She reached into her Mary Poppins hold-all purse and pulled out a piece of soft brown fabric in a houndstooth pattern. "It's an eternity scarf," Iris told me, looping it stylishly around my neck. "Perfect for fall. I finished it in sewing and needlecraft yesterday. With a special little accent for my favorite detective." She pulled out one section of the scarf to expose a small metal pin—made with a wire, beads, and a little disc of glass.

"A magnifying glass!" I exclaimed. "Oh, Iris, I love it!"

"Wear it in good health, Sherlock," she said, giving me one last breathtaking squeeze. "And the next time you're chasing some baddie down a deserted street in the middle of the night—do me a favor."

"What's that?" I asked.

"Wear sneakers!"

Dear Diary,

IT SURE IS GOOD TO BE HOME! I JUST spent the entire afternoon hanging out with George and Bess, and they demanded I tell them *everything*. It took quite a while, but they got the whole crazy story. I'm so glad that everything with Bash and Dr. Stone turned out all right—I have a feeling that the classics department is in very good hands. I also got to show off my fancy new sleuthing scarf, which Bess raved over. She said it looked perfect with my red hair. Who knew that detective work could be so stylish?

New mystery. New suspense. New danger.

Nancy Drew
DIARIES™

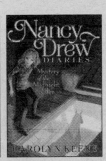

BY CAROLYN KEENE

EBOOK EDITIONS ALSO AVAILABLE   From Aladdin | simonandschuster.com/kids

Looking for another great book?
Find it
IN THE MIDDLE.

Fun, fantastic books for kids
in the in-beTWEEN age.

IntheMiddleBooks.com

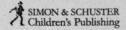 SIMON & SCHUSTER
Children's Publishing   /SimonKids 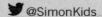 @SimonKids

New mystery. New suspense. New danger.

HARDYBOYS ADVENTURES™

BY FRANKLIN W. DIXON

EBOOK EDITIONS ALSO AVAILABLE   From Aladdin | simonandschuster.com/kids